"Remember—I had you in my bed and didn't lay a finger on you."

"That's true," admitted Kate.

Philip looked at her with an intent searching gaze that seemed to strip her naked. Then he raised his fingers and touched her gently under the chin.

"So can't you accept that I was carried away when I kissed you, just as you were?" he asked.

Kate swallowed, acutely conscious of his featherlike touch. Reaching up her own hand, she moved his fingers away.

"Even if you were, then where does that leave us?" she retorted bitterly. "All right, so we felt a mutual attraction, but there's no future in it, is there?"

Philip's eyes blazed defiantly. "I'm not so sure about that."

ANGELA DEVINE grew up in Tasmania, surrounded by forests, mountains and wild seas—it's no
wonder she's not a fan of big cities. Before taking up
writing, she worked as a teacher, librarian and uni-
versity lecturer. As a young mother and Ph.D. student, she read romance fiction for enjoyment and
later decided it would be even more fun to write.
Angela is married with four children, loves chocolate and Twinings tea, and hates ironing. Her current hobbies include gardening, bushwalking,
traveling and listening to classical music.

ANGELA DEVINE

Wife for a Night

Harlequin Books

TORONTO • NEW YORK • LONDON
AMSTERDAM • PARIS • SYDNEY • HAMBURG
STOCKHOLM • ATHENS • TOKYO • MILAN
MADRID • WARSAW • BUDAPEST • AUCKLAND

Harlequin Presents first edition March 1993
ISBN 0-373-11538-5

Original hardcover edition published in 1991
by Mills & Boon Limited

WIFE FOR A NIGHT

CHAPTER ONE

'HELP! Help! *Voethia!*'

Kate shouted with all her might and waved her torch despairingly at the glossy white car that was nosing its way down the mountain road in the gathering twilight. Let him stop, please, please, please let him stop, she thought urgently. A convulsive shiver ran through her and she gripped the torch harder, suddenly aware that she was close to panic. She was twenty-six years old and not much given to panic in general, but then she had never been through an earthquake before. Her work as a photographer had put her in some very tight spots, but this had to be the worst yet. Scrambling down a mountainside that quivered like jelly under her feet with stones crashing down around her was not an experience she wanted to repeat. And finding her hire-car wrecked beyond any possible hope of driving was even worse. For over an hour she had been sitting here, fighting down her terror of another quake. Now the hope of rescue was unbearably tantalising. She swung the torch in a wild arc and shouted again.

'*Voethia!*'

The car paused suddenly in its cautious downward course, and Kate caught her breath with relief. Then, just as suddenly, it continued over the edge of the slope and disappeared out of sight. It was all she could do not to burst into tears. Dropping her camera case, she scrambled through the mass of fallen rocks and ran to the bend where the road disappeared from view. The sight which met her eyes was typical of the wild and lonely Halkidiki region of northern Greece. All she could see was the pale ribbon of the road looping down a series

5

of hairpin bends to the floor of the valley far below. A
river cut like a silver scimitar through the dark landscape, and tall stands of pine trees reared their battle-
ments against the fading red glow of the sunset, but there
was no sign of life anywhere. The car had vanished as
if it had never existed, hidden no doubt by one of the
outcrops of rock far below.

'Damn!' said Kate. 'Damn, damn, damn. I'll just have
to camp out for the night. Oh, why do these things always
happen to me?'

Picking her way back to her own car, she shone the
torch on it and frowned thoughtfully. It wasn't a reassuring sight. A large rock had smashed the wind-
screen, sending shards of glass all over the front seat,
and another rock had dented the roof. But would the
car offer her the best hope of shelter for the night or
should she camp out under a heavy rock ledge? She
hauled a woven Greek rug out of the back seat and
paused uncertainly. If another quake came, which would
be worse?

'Oh, I wish the ground would open up and swallow
that awful man in the white car!' she declared
passionately.

'How very uncivilised of you!' said a deep, throaty
voice with an undercurrent of amusement. The accent
was faintly Greek, but the words were English.

Kate spun round with a gasp and saw a figure looming
over her in the twilight. Snatching up her torch, she
played its beam on the man's face. He must have been
in his mid-thirties and, although not conventionally
handsome, he was certainly striking in looks. Glossy dark
hair sprang in waves above features she had seen a
thousand times on Greek vases. Liquid brown eyes narrowed against the light; a short, straight nose; full, sen-
suous lips, twitching with the effort not to smile. His
frame was taut and muscular and he wore grey trousers
and an open-necked white shirt, which revealed a gold

neck-chain and a tuft of springy dark hair on his chest. Yet, in spite of the casual clothes, something about him suggested wealth and power·and assurance. Perhaps it was his aura of having the whole situation totally under control. With a sigh Kate felt some of the tension drain out of her.

'Why did you leave me?' she demanded bluntly.

'I didn't,' he replied, still with that undercurrent of amusement. 'It was merely a strategic withdrawal. I thought it best to park the car under a rock ledge, which would give it some protection in the event of another quake. These things are rather unpredictable, you realise. It could happen at any moment.'

Another convulsive shiver hit Kate.

'I know,' she said through clenched teeth.

'You're cold and frightened,' he murmured in a voice full of concern. 'Come, we'll get your things and go to my car. With luck we may be able to make it through to the next village. If not, my car should at least be more comfortable for camping than yours.'

That much was certainly true, thought Kate in amazement as they reached the spot where the white car sat snugly hidden under a rock ledge. Her rescuer opened the passenger-door, revealing an interior so luxurious that she could do nothing but gape. The seats were of brown leather, and a car phone was tossed idly on one of them, alongside a slender dark briefcase and a Louis Vuitton overnight bag. She felt suddenly conscious of the shabbiness of her own holdall and stained camera bag dangling easily from his lean, brown hands, then he opened the boot and thrust them swiftly out of sight.

'Now,' he said with satisfaction, 'in you get. The torch you may put in the glove-box. The rug, I think, you would be well advised to keep around you. You may be suffering from delayed shock. And I'll dress that cut on your head for you before we go.'

'Cut?' asked Kate blankly.

'On your temple. Weren't you aware of it?'

'No, I wasn't,' she said stupidly.

His fingers were firm and reassuring as he set to work. From somewhere in the car's gleaming interior he produced a first-aid box, and Kate felt the sting of antiseptic, followed by the smoothness of a healing cream and the pressure of sticking plaster. Warmth seemed to lap over her in waves, and she pulled the rug around her and leant back against the seat, luxuriating in the feeling of being safe and cosseted. Whoever this man was, he was amazingly calm and competent. It did not even surprise her when he produced a stylish white Thermos flask and pressed a cup of hot, sweet Turkish coffee into her hands.

'Thank you,' she said gratefully. 'You really are the most astonishing person, Mr...?'

'Andronikos. Philip Andronikos. And you are Miss...?'

'Katherine. Katherine Walsh. But I'm usually called Kate.'

'Kate?' He tried the monosyllable on his tongue, wrinkling his face distastefully. 'It seems to me a very ugly abbreviation, not at all suitable for a beautiful young woman. I will call you Katarina.'

Kate ran her fingers through her feathery auburn curls and choked on a giggle.

'Something I have said amuses you?'

'I'm sorry. It's just the way you called me a beautiful young woman. I don't feel in the least bit beautiful. I fell over at least half a dozen times getting down the mountainside, my jeans are ripped to shreds and my shirt is filthy.'

'Ah, yes. Your clothes are atrocious, I grant you, and they must have been dreadful even before you ruined them. But that oval face and the emerald-green eyes and the red hair...I stand by my statement, Miss Walsh. You are a beautiful young woman.'

Kate wriggled uncomfortably.

'What else should I wear on a mountainside if not jeans and a shirt?' she asked, feeling unaccountably annoyed by his comment.

'Ah, you English!' he exclaimed. 'Why is it that you cannot accept a compliment gracefully? I tell you how beautiful you are and you complain because I do not like your clothes.'

'I'm not English,' protested Kate irrelevantly. 'I'm Australian!'

'Very well, Australian, then. And for the sake of peace I will even admit that your clothes were extremely suitable for scrambling about on a lonely mountain. But whatever were you doing there in the first place?'

'Taking photos,' said Kate pertly. 'What were you doing there?'

He smiled at the hint of annoyance in her voice.

'I'm a hotel developer,' he said. 'I was on my way back to my newest hotel in Sithoniá and I chose the scenic route through the mountains. Fortunately for you, perhaps.'

'Yes,' admitted Kate reluctantly. She took a swift gulp of the hot coffee and gave him a wavering smile. 'I can't tell you how pleased I was to see you coming down the hill, Mr Andronikos. For a moment there I really thought that...'

Her voice broke and she could not continue. A gleam of compassion came into his eyes and his lean, brown fingers reached out and touched her tumbled hair.

'You're safe now, Katarina,' he said softly. 'And in the circumstances I think we should drop this Mr Andronikos stuff. My name is Philip. OK?'

'OK,' she agreed with a touch of spirit.

'Good. Then finish your coffee and we'll get moving. Where were you headed for before the quake struck?'

'Nyssa. It's a village about eighty kilometres from here. Do you know it?'

'Yes. I doubt if we'll get that far, but at least we can try.'

A moment later she handed him her empty cup, which he stowed in a bag in the back seat. Then he fastened his seatbelt and turned on the ignition.

'I intend to go very slowly,' he explained. 'I've been in touch with my secretary on the radio phone ever since the quake started and he's given me as much information as he can. As far as I know, the road is clear from here to Pirgadikia, but there will almost certainly be some rocks on the way. Now tell me about these photos. You are a professional photographer, are you not?'

'Yes,' agreed Kate curiously. 'How did you know?'

'My dear Katarina, it is obvious. You have two hundred thousand drachmas' worth of photographic equipment in that bag. Your other luggage is not worth a tenth of that amount. Either you are a complete fool about spending your money or you are a very serious photographer. So what were you photographing? The scenery?'

'No. I was taking some photos of an archaeological site for someone I've been staying with. An archaeologist I met a few weeks ago in Turkey. Dr Charlie Lucas, the head of the team at Nyssa.'

His eyebrows flew up.

'Late on a Sunday afternoon in a remote area on your own? Don't you realise there are wolves in these mountains? Not to mention the danger of an accident occurring or some man finding you alone and unprotected! But I suppose that wouldn't worry you if you're prepared to stay with a man you met only a few weeks ago. Anyway, what was this Dr Lucas of yours doing that he could not accompany you?'

His voice was harsh with disapproval. Looking at his chiselled profile, Kate felt a sudden rush of annoyance.

'If you must know what Dr Lucas was doing, she was washing her clothes. She, not he. Charlotte Elizabeth Lucas, better known as Charlie. She's hoping to excavate here at Mount Panagia next summer and she asked me to take some preliminary photos of the site for her. At the moment she's digging near Nyssa, and I've been with her there for the last two weeks. Although I don't see that it's really any business of yours who I stay with!'

'Hmm,' said Philip suspiciously. 'But, even if it had been a man, you would still have stayed with him, wouldn't you?'

'Probably,' agreed Kate. 'If he had offered me work and if I trusted him. Why shouldn't I?'

'Because your honour would be compromised,' replied Philip earnestly.

Kate choked on a disbelieving laugh.

'You really mean that, don't you?' she demanded.

'Of course,' agreed Philip emphatically. 'But I don't want to quarrel with you. Tell me about your photos. Why couldn't you take them during the week when other people were with you?'

'Today is the first day that the light has been exactly right,' replied Kate, glad of the change of subject.

The amusement was back in his tone.

'And the light must be exactly right? So you are a perfectionist, Katarina?'

'You could say that.'

'And do you only work on archaeological sites or do you do other types of photography as well?'

'Anything, really,' said Kate. 'I'm trying to get established as a freelance photographer, so I take whatever work is available. Shop catalogues, photojournalism, anything. But my favourite work is what I suppose you'd call artistic photography. Landscapes, studies of light and shade, visual images that I find evocative.'

'But why come to Greece to be a photographer? Couldn't you have done it in Australia?'

She bit her lip thoughtfully.

'Yes and no,' she said. 'I did try to get established in Australia. In fact I had a job as a video-camerawoman with a Sydney TV station, but after three years I was retrenched. At first I was so stunned that I didn't know which way to turn.'

'Couldn't your family help you?' asked Philip.

Kate made a face.

'Actually, they did try,' she admitted. 'My father's a solicitor and he invited me to come back to the country town where they live and work as his secretary, but I couldn't bear to take help from them. They never really wanted me to become a photographer and I knew they'd only end up gloating. So I drew out all my savings and came to Europe.'

'Some people would call that a very rash move,' said Philip critically.

Kate's chin came up defiantly and her eyes flashed.

'Sometimes you have to take rash moves if you don't want to settle for second best in your life,' she retorted.

Philip's stern features relaxed into a reluctant smile.

'You're a woman after my own heart,' he said admiringly. 'Even if you are a foreigner.'

'What have you got against foreigners?' asked Kate challengingly.

Philip stared fiercely ahead at the road plummeting away in front of them, as if he could force a passage through the obstacles by sheer will-power.

'I don't approve of their morals,' he said half to himself. 'I lived in England for three years and I was shocked by the way young people rushed into casual relationships. Especially the girls. No dowries, no commitment, no way of knowing where they stood. In my opinion all this talk of freedom means nothing more than self-indulgence for men, and suffering for women.'

Kate had been all ready to argue hotly with him, but now she bit her lip and remained silent. If she was honest,

Philip's outburst struck a chord with her. Certainly her brief, disastrous affair with the glamorous English current-affairs reporter Leon Clark had fitted the description pretty closely. Self-indulgence for Leon, suffering for her. Swallowing the lump in her throat, she turned her head and stared unseeingly at the dark blue twilight outside the car.

He simply put out one lean brown hand and covered her fingers with his.

'I've upset you. I apologise,' he said frankly, his eyes still fixed on the dark road ahead.

She was silent, feeling strangely moved and comforted by that warm clasp. An impulse ran through her to confide in Philip and ask him what to do. Should she go home now while she still had some emergency funds left, or wait until her meagre finances dried up completely? Something about him urged her to lay all her problems in his lap and wait for a solution, but pride reasserted itself. She had been enough of a wimp already today without blurting out her little saga of how hard it was to break into professional photography. Gritting her teeth, she gazed out at the dark outlines of the pine trees that flanked the road. Philip's hand moved back to the steering-wheel as if he had been stung.

'You do not say anything, Katarina. Did I hurt your feelings with my attack on foreign morals?'

Kate hesitated. But there seemed little point in crying on Philip's shoulder about how shabbily Leon had treated her. Simpler just to let him think she was offended and leave it at that.

'Yes,' she said tersely. 'I can't say I enjoyed being scared out of my wits by the earthquake and then lectured by you into the bargain.'

'It is just that I see everything through Greek eyes,' Philip explained. 'We are very protective towards our women. It would be almost inconceivable for a Greek woman to find herself alone in such a dangerous situation as you were in today.'

Kate's lips quivered.

'Just for tonight I'm finding it very pleasant indeed to be a Greek woman,' she assured him. 'There's nothing I'd like better at the moment than simply to give up and lean on you.'

Philip's fingers moved back to the blanket, tucked it below her chin, then touched her cheek in a fleeting caress.

'Then do it,' he urged. 'You've had a very frightening time. Why don't you just go to sleep and let me deal with the problems from now on?'

How long she slept Kate did not know, but when she woke she was vaguely conscious of the barking of dogs and a narrow lamplit street flanked by shuttered white houses. Gazing around her, she saw that Philip was gone and panic surged through her. But, as she struggled out of the rug, he came out of one of the whitewashed houses and crossed the street towards her. A sign on the door said *'domatia enoikiazontai'*. Rooms to let, thought Kate with sudden comprehension as Philip opened the car door.

'Good, you're awake,' he said. 'This is Ayía Sofía. I'm afraid we can't go any further tonight—the road ahead is blocked. But I've found a place to stay. It's fairly primitive but quite clean. There's only one problem.'

'What's that?' asked Kate, groping in the glove-box for her torch.

'There's only one room available.'

He made this pronouncement with such gravity that Kate felt an irrepressible impulse to burst out laughing.

'Honestly, Philip!' she exclaimed. 'I thought you were going to tell me there was another earthquake on the way at the very least. I don't mind sharing a room with you. It's not the first time I've had to share with a man when I've been travelling. It really doesn't bother me.'

His mouth hardened.

'I think I would prefer that it did,' he said disapprovingly. 'Somehow I do not like the idea of your sharing rooms so eagerly with other men. But, as I said before, foreign morals are very peculiar to me. You tourists come here and sleep with men you hardly know, but I can't pretend I approve of it.'

'Now, just a minute!' exclaimed Kate hotly. 'When I said "share a room", that's all I meant. Not "share a bed", whatever you may choose to think. I don't suppose you've ever been young and poor, but it's the only way a lot of people can afford to travel.'

Philip's eyebrows rose sceptically.

'Perhaps,' he said fastidiously. 'But it is not a custom I care for. However, tonight there seems to be no choice. I have told the woman in the house that you are my wife and you will be treated with the greatest respect. And, needless to say, your honour will be safe in my keeping.'

He gave a small, formal nod as he said this and reached out his hand to help Kate out of the car. As their fingers met she was conscious of a warm current like electricity tingling between them, and the question shot irresistibly through her mind. What would it really be like to be Philip Andronikos's wife? She had no doubt that he would be protective and considerate. But wouldn't he also be arrogant and intensely jealous? Somehow the idea did not repel her in the way she'd expected. Instead it sent an odd, heady excitement coursing through her veins so that she gave an involuntary shiver.

'You're cold,' said Philip swiftly, draping the rug around her shoulders. 'Go inside while I get the bags.'

A dark-haired woman, whose smile glinted with gold, came forward to greet Kate. With obvious pride she showed the girl a tiny bathroom with a flush toilet and overhead shower. Then she led her through into a bedroom, which was scrupulously clean but had as its only furniture a wardrobe, a chair, a bedside table and a very small double bed. Kate swallowed. Suddenly she didn't feel nearly so blasé about sharing a room with Philip. One of them would have to sleep on the floor, she decided, gazing wildly around her. The woman caught her anxious glance.

'*Endaxi?*' she asked.

'*Ne. Ne. Endaxi,*' agreed Kate, smiling desperately. It's fine. Or at least it would be if we really were married or desperately in love. But the floor is terrazzo, it'll be hideously cold and uncomfortable, apart from being cramped. I can't possibly expect Philip to sleep there. Then I'll have to.

She became suddenly aware of the woman's puzzled look. '*Endaxi,*' she repeated desperately.

Reassured, the woman withdrew amid an absolute torrent of Greek and a good deal of mime, designed to assure Kate that a meal would soon appear. Left alone, Kate looked nervously around her. There were two windows, each hung with a rectangle of handmade lace, and in front of each was a garish vase of plastic flowers. The walls were whitewashed and must have been well over a foot thick, judging by the depth of the windowsills. The room had no decoration apart from the flowers, an icon of the Virgin Mary, hanging above the bed, and a green and white woven rug on the floor. Kate found her gaze drawn irresistibly back to that bed. The crisp white sheets and the fluffy blanket with its pattern of pink roses seemed somehow indefinably threatening. Or exciting. She wasn't sure which. In an effort to come to grips with the strange emotion that filled her, she seized one of the white pillows and set it down on the floor in the corner furthest from the bed. Then she moved the green and white rug into the corner and laid her own rug on top of it. There. At least she had made herself a separate bed.

'What on earth do you think you're doing?' demanded a familiar voice behind her.

Kate spun round.

'Oh, Philip. I was just making up another bed.'

Philip gave a contemptuous snort of laughter.

'I am not sleeping on the floor,' he said in a low, throaty voice.

'No, not for you! For me! What...what are you doing?'

Without a word Philip seized the pillow, dusted it off briskly and replaced it on the double bed. Then he kicked one rug into place, folded the other and set it in a corner, and smiled charmingly at Kate.

'Now some dinner, I think. But you will want a wash first, won't you?'

'Philip! You...you've just destroyed the bed I made. Why? Why did you do it?'

He looked at her appraisingly, but said nothing. A slow smile spread over his face, as if he thought the whole subject too absurd to comment on. Then, whistling softly to himself, he began to unpack his overnight bag and set his toiletries on the bedside table. Furious at being so rudely ignored, Kate snatched up the pillow she had just set down. To her rage and disbelief, she found her wrist caught and held.

'What do you think you are doing, Katarina?' Philip's voice was low and threatening.

'Making up my bed,' she said through her teeth.

'Oh, no, you're not,' he said softly. 'You are sleeping with me.'

Cold chills of panic and excitement chased one another up Kate's spine at these words. Then a warm, treacherous wave of desire flooded through her.

'I thought you said my honour was safe with you,' she said challengingly.

'And just suppose it isn't?' demanded Philip.

Shock, outrage and a tremor of anticipation went through her. She looked at his dark, brooding face and felt an overwhelming urge simply to open her arms to him and let him take her. Shame coursed through her at the thought. She was every bit as bad as the tourists he had been denouncing. After all, she had only just met him and she knew nothing about him. Her eyelashes fluttered as she blinked back tears.

'Philip...you wouldn't,' she said in a tremulous voice.

He took the pillow from her nerveless fingers and laid it neatly on the bed. Then his arms came round her. Warm and safe and reassuring, but with a hint of steel in them.

'No, I wouldn't,' he said huskily. 'But supposing I did decide to? What do you think you could do to prevent me, down there on your concrete slab? If I chose to possess you, couldn't I simply take you?'

She was silent, conscious of the thudding of her heart, of the warm, spicy scent of his aftershave lotion, of an urgent longing that was spreading all through her, driving the blood into the tips of her fingers.

His arms tightened around her. 'Couldn't I?' he insisted.

'Yes,' she whispered.

She knew then that he was going to kiss her. And it was every bit as powerful and overwhelming as she had feared. His deft fingers tilted her chin and his mouth came down on hers with a deep, passionate tenderness that left her aching for more. Her bones seemed to melt beneath his touch as his sensitive hands moved caressingly down over her shoulders and back, moulding her against the warm, muscular strength of his body. She uttered a small whimper of longing and let herself relax into the passionate certainty of his embrace. For an instant she felt the sudden flare of excitement that coursed through him, then he thrust her roughly away from him. His breath came in a swift, shallow gasp as he unclenched his fingers from her shirt and she could see the rapid throbbing of the pulse in his neck.

'Don't think I'm not tempted,' he said hoarsely as he released her. 'But you'll be as safe with me in the bed as on the floor, and a good deal more comfortable. Besides, Kyria Georgia is sure to be coming in and out of the room with coffee and such. I don't want her thinking I can't control my own wife.'

Kate laughed, caught between amusement and outrage.

'Supposing I really were your wife and we had quarrelled?' she demanded.

His brows drew together.

'Then the quarrel would most definitely be settled in bed,' he said with authority. 'Now go and have your shower.'

The shower was only tepid, but it was wonderfully refreshing after the rigours of the afternoon. Kate shampooed her hair and lathered herself vigorously with soap to try and get rid of the grime from the mountainside. The bathroom was so tiny that she almost needed to be a contortionist to get dressed in it, but somehow she achieved the feat. And vanity made her put on her one decent outfit. A crush-proof jade-green and white pleated skirt with a crisp white blouse and cardigan.

Even so, she realised that she was hopelessly outclassed when Kyria Georgia showed her out on to a vine-clad terrace lit by a single lamp. Philip too had changed, and his fashionable navy sports jacket, striped shirt and grey trousers bore the unmistakable imprint of expensive tailoring. He rose to his feet as she appeared and strode towards her. Kyria Georgia smiled fondly as he dropped a swift kiss on Kate's cheek and led her to the edge of the terrace.

'Don't stiffen like that,' he chided. 'You're my wife, remember, and Kyria Georgia is having a wonderful time reliving her youth as she watches us. She particularly wants me to show you the romantic view over the sea.'

It was romantic, no question about that. The house was set on a hill-top, and down below the other dwellings of the village clustered together, like a flock of timid white chickens, surrounded by silver olive groves. Behind the village was a vast amphitheatre of rocky cliffs, bathed in moonlight, and in the distance was the silvery, shimmering surface of the sea. As Philip's hand rested casually on her shoulder Kate felt a hungry pang of longing dart through her. But what she was longing for, she really could not say.

'*Kali oreksi,*' said the *kyria*, setting out the last of the dishes and withdrawing with another beaming smile.

'*Kali oreksi?*' asked Kate in a baffled voice.

Philip pulled back her chair for her and smiled.

'It means "good appetite",' he explained. 'And I hope your appetite is good, because she'll be mortally offended if we don't eat every scrap of this.'

'In that case I'll consider it my duty to make a perfect pig of myself,' said Kate, twinkling at him. 'Anyway, it looks delicious.'

It was delicious. The water jug and a bottle of retsina wine stood huddled in the middle of the table surrounded by a positive banquet of hearty peasant food. There was a wicker basket of crusty bread, various dips made of aubergine and smoked cod's roe, a salad of feta cheese, Spanish onions, black olives, tomatoes and cucumber and a main dish of souvlaki on skewers with fried potatoes. When the *kyria* brought in a plate of sticky baklava and Turkish coffee to finish, she smiled approvingly at the inroads they had made on the meal.

After a long, exhausting and rather frightening day, Kate was content to sit in silence, sipping her coffee and gazing down at the silvery sea. Inside the living-room, Kyria Georgia switched on a radio and the haunting rhythms of Greek dance music swirled out across the terrace. An impulse to laugh and dance and cry swept over Kate, and she gave a small, ragged sigh. Philip looked at her questioningly.

'What is it?' he asked.

She spread her hands, unable to explain adequately.

'Just one of those moments of magic,' she said with a self-conscious smile. 'It's such a beautiful evening, the meal was delicious, and now there's this music that makes me feel like dancing. Sometimes I think I'm awfully lucky just to be alive.'

He gazed at her indulgently.

'Are you really so easily pleased?' he asked disbelievingly. 'Some women I know would be insulted if they were asked to stay in such a humble place and eat such a simple meal.'

'Then some women just don't know how to enjoy themselves,' retorted Kate.

Philip's liquid brown eyes rested searchingly on her face.

'Sometimes, when I've been working in the city with the noise and the crowds and the so-called sophistication, I feel a desperate need to escape,' he said thoughtfully. 'When that happens I just abandon the city and flee to some place like this that's simple and wholesome. Deep down I think that's what I crave most. But I can't help wondering sometimes whether women aren't rather like cities.'

Kate frowned in bewilderment.

'What do you mean?' she asked.

'Perhaps there are two kinds,' he said cryptically. 'One is fast, noisy and sophisticated. The other is simple and wholesome. Do you want to dance, Katarina?'

When she rose from her seat she stumbled, and he had to catch her arm to save her from falling.

'I'm sorry,' she said. 'It must be the retsina. I'm not used to drinking it.'

'Two glasses can't have hurt you,' replied Philip with a smile. 'It will be just enough to make you relax and go with the music. Now hold on to my hand and let me guide you.'

A moment later she was stumbling through the steps, certain that she would never be able to match her movements to his. But a moment after that she saw that he was right. Something seemed to click into place, and suddenly she was moving effortlessly in step with Philip, her feet going faster and faster as she followed him through the intricate patterns of the dance. First to the left, then to the right and finally in dizzy circles that left her breathless and laughing as the music came to an end.

'Bravo!' said Philip admiringly. 'I think you must be a true Greek at heart, Katarina. Now come and sit down and get your breath back.'

Kate collapsed into a chair and fanned herself vigorously with a paper napkin.

'I love Greek music!' she exclaimed. 'I only hope I'll get a chance to hear some live bouzouki-playing before I leave the country.'

'Really?' asked Philip with interest. 'If I had a bouzouki here I could grant your wish right away. I used to play a little when I was younger, although I'm a bit rusty now.'

'There's a bouzouki on top of the cupboard in the living-room,' said Kate. 'I wonder if Kyria Georgia would lend it to you. Why don't you go and ask her?'

Philip hesitated.

'I haven't played for a couple of years,' he confessed.

'Go on,' urged Kate. 'I'd love to hear you, and I promise I won't be critical.'

With an eagerness he could scarcely conceal Philip went back into the house. The radio music ceased and, after a couple of minutes, he came back out on to the terrace with the bouzouki in his hands. Kate could not help noticing how he caressed the honey-gold wood of the instrument with loving fingers, almost as if he were fondling a woman. He played a couple of minor chords, his head bent thoughtfully to catch the sound.

'What would you like to hear?' he asked.

'Do you know anything by Xarhakos?' asked Kate.

Philip hummed a few bars of 'Poverty' and looked at her questioningly. She nodded approval and, with a suddenness that shocked and enthralled her, the bouzouki leapt into life. Philip played like a man possessed, with a fire and passion that made Kate feel she was being swept along on a wild current of sound. When the last, lingering cadence died away she stared at him, speechless with emotion.

'Well?' he asked offhandedly.

Kate saw that his nonchalance concealed a profound urgency. Obviously her opinion really mattered to him.

'Surely you don't need to ask me?' she said slowly. 'It was magnificent, Philip. Utterly magnificent. I've never been so moved in my life.'

'Truly?' he demanded.

'Truly.'

'Let me play you a love-song,' he suggested. 'I'd like to know your opinion of it.'

This time the music was quieter, softer, more haunting. It stirred a poignant memory in Kate's breast. A memory of an achingly sweet evening in a Greek restaurant in Sydney that had turned to ashes. The evening when Leon Clark had broken the news that he was already married. Tears gathered in her eyes and she had to bite her lip as Philip's low, husky voice sang the lyrics of love and yearning. Swallowing hard, she turned her head away as the song came to an end and Philip set down the bouzouki.

'Katarina?'

She was silent, too overwhelmed to speak. Then she felt his powerful fingers grip her shoulder as he turned her to face him. Horrified, he saw the tears gleaming on her lashes.

'What is it? I've upset you, haven't I? I'm a brute, a fool! I should never have played this stupid instrument!'

'No! No, Philip. You're no brute, you're an artist. It's just that you brought back...memories.'

'Of a man who hurt you?' he asked shrewdly.

She nodded, blinking back the tears. His hand came up and touched her face. Then with a low groan of emotion he threaded his fingers through her flame-coloured hair and drew her in hard against him. She could feel the tempestuous thudding of his heart, the rapid rhythmic rise and fall of his breathing, the warmth radiating out from his body.

'Oh, *agapimou*,' he sighed. 'You wake a part of me that I thought was gone forever.'

This time his kiss was as gentle as the opening of a flower. Her lips trembled as he raised her mouth to his, and for an instant she clung to him, feeling as if she had found a safe haven. Then the warm flame of yearning in his eyes made her suddenly self-conscious. She had never before met a man who made her feel all woman as she did at this moment. Tender, aching, vulnerable. She sat there, twisting her fingers together, unaware that her feelings showed so clearly in her face. Desperately she fought to remain impassive. This is ridiculous, she told herself. I'll never see him after tomorrow. The thought stiffened her pride.

'Thank you for a lovely evening, Philip,' she said formally. 'If you'll excuse me I think I'll go to bed now.'

Sensing her change of mood, he helped her to her feet without comment and stood aside to let her pass.

'Goodnight, Katarina,' he replied. '*Kalinichta*. I won't come in until you're asleep and I won't disturb you. You have my word for that. Oh, and I meant to ask you—do you have any of your photos with you that I could look at?'

'Of course,' she said, feeling suddenly shy. 'They're in my bag in the bedroom. I'll get them for you.'

After Kate had left him alone with the photos Philip opened the folder and began to flick through its contents. At first he gazed idly, and then with mounting interest. Soon he was spreading the prints out on the table, looking at them from different angles and pursing his lips thoughtfully. Eventually he poured himself a glass of ouzo and sipped it slowly. For more than two hours he sat on the terrace, drumming his fingers on the tabletop and staring out at the moonlit sea. Shortly after midnight he went inside the house and fetched his briefcase. Then he set some documents and a photograph out on the table and brooded over them for a long time. At last, with an exclamation of impatience, he flung them into the briefcase and slammed the lid. Striding inside, he opened the bedroom door.

'Katarina?' he whispered softly.

Stirring in her sleep, she made a faint sound like the purring of a kitten. The darkness was soft and velvety around her, and she wasn't sure whether she dreamt or felt that faint brush of warm lips against her cheek. So faint that it was no more than a butterfly's touch.

'Goodnight, Katarina,' said Philip.

CHAPTER TWO

KATE woke from a deep and dreamless sleep to the sound of clucking chickens and distant voices. An arrow of sunlight slanted through a gap in the curtains and lit up a blanket with an unfamiliar pattern of pink roses. For a moment she was baffled, then it all came rushing back to her. The earthquake, her meeting with Philip... Colour rushed into her face and she turned over shyly, stretching out her hand. But the bed was empty. Philip had gone.

A flood of contradictory feelings swept over Kate at this realisation. Relief, disappointment, annoyance, disbelief. Then reason reasserted itself. Philip wouldn't just leave her like that; she knew he wouldn't. He was probably only in the bathroom or out on the terrace. But something drew her gaze inexorably to the bedside table, and she saw that it was empty. Sitting up, she stared bleakly around the room. Every trace of him was gone. His toiletries, his clothes, the dark briefcase, the Louis Vuitton overnight bag. He had vanished as completely as if he had never existed.

The discovery sent shock waves through her. Somehow, even in the few short hours she had known him, she had come to depend on Philip Andronikos. The common danger of the earthquake had plunged them into an intimate relationship of trust and sharing, but she would have sworn that there was more to it than that. No man had ever kissed her as Philip had done last night, igniting a flame that still seemed to rage inside her. She had never known a man at once so irresistible and so infuriating. Arrogant, domineering, disdainful and yet warm, protective and passionate. He kissed me as if he really cared, thought Kate miserably, and now he's gone! And how on earth am I to get away from this village? The hire-car is smashed up and I've hardly any money left... Her anxious thoughts were interrupted by a knock at the door.

'Come in,' she called, unable to recall even a syllable of the simplest Greek.

Kyria Georgia came sailing through the doorway with a beaming smile and a tray laden with coffee and rolls.

'*Kalimera,*' she said cheerfully.

'*Kalimera,*' replied Kate despondently, knowing that she must ask an extremely awkward question.

Her mind raced as she groped for the right words. How on earth could she ask this woman where Philip had gone? Wouldn't the Kyria simply be shocked that she didn't know about her own husband's movements? And, even supposing the older woman did know where he was, would Kate's abysmal Greek be good enough to understand her answer?

'*O... sizighos mou?*' she stammered. 'My husband?'

'*Ne, ne!*'

The woman nodded, smiled and indicated that Kate should drink her coffee. Then she rushed from the room and returned with a letter, which she laid on the tray. With a final, encouraging pat on Kate's shoulder, she swept out of the room to deal with the hens, which had strayed on to the terrace. Sighing with relief, Kate leant back against the pillows and took a gulp of strong, sweet Turkish coffee to steady her. Then, setting down her cup, she tackled Philip's letter.

The envelope was plain, of good quality and addressed simply to 'Katarina'. As she tore it open a small wad of banknotes and a single folded sheet of paper dropped on to the blanket. Baffled, she put the money aside and unfolded the letter. It said simply,

Sorry to rush off. Urgent business in Thessaloníki. Road open, bill already paid and your car repairs organised. Left you cash for emergencies. Philip.

A wave of disappointment swept through her. Well, what did you expect? she asked herself savagely. A proposal of marriage? No, not that, she admitted, but something. Some indication that he too had felt that powerful current of attraction and understanding between them, just as she had. An invitation to dinner, a request for her address at the dig. Something. But it hadn't happened.

'You're on your own now, Kate Walsh,' she said aloud. 'And don't you forget it.'

Three days later Kate was moping on the terrace of a house in Nyssa. All around her was the controlled chaos typical of the headquarters of an archaeological site. Four of the local Greek women were washing potsherds in large plastic bowls of soapy water, a couple of Australian girls were sorting pottery fragments on a wire-mesh table, and a lanky young man was balanced on top of a ladder, struggling to tie a plastic canopy over the vine-clad pergola. Kate herself was half-heartedly drawing a large pottery bead, but her thoughts kept straying. Now that the photos were finished there was really no reason for her to stay on any longer. She simply must make a decision either to look for another job or go home to Australia. Philip Andronikos had gone out of her life as abruptly as he had entered it, and she knew perfectly well that she would never see him again. So why couldn't she stop thinking about him?

'Kate!'

'Yes?'

Kate looked up idly as one of the other team members called her. Naomi had tired of sorting pottery and was flicking through a glossy American magazine.

'What did you say was the name of that Greek chap who rescued you on the mountain?'

'Philip. Philip Andronikos.'

Strange how even saying his name should send that odd thrill of excitement through her!

'Is this him? Look, there's a photo here of some filthy rich Greek hotel developer, and the name is exactly the same. I suppose it's just a coincidence, but wouldn't it be funny if it was the same guy?'

'Let me see.'

Naomi lounged across the terrace and set the magazine down on the table. For a moment the world seemed to stand still. With a shock of pleasure and recognition Kate saw Philip's dark eyes glaring back at her from the photo, as if the photographer's intrusion had enraged him. Then shock of a different kind assaulted her. For Philip's hand was resting on the arm of a glamorous, dark-haired siren of a woman, and underneath the photo was a casual but devastating caption.

Hotel magnate Philip Andronikos and his beautiful fiancée Irene Marmara enjoy Sunday brunch at the Athens Hilton hotel. Rumour has it that Andronikos, who recently completed a new luxury hotel in the Halkidiki region, has plans for even greater expansion after his marriage. He is believed to be on the brink of venturing into a complex project involving vineyards, agricultural estates and tourist units in the Sithoniá peninsula...

For an instant Kate stood perfectly still. There was a roaring noise in her ears, and the chatter of the Greek women seemed to recede into the distance. So that was it, she thought. A fiancée tucked away in the background. No wonder he vanished over the horizon before I even woke up! And now I'll never see him again. She wanted to cry, rage, scream. But to her amazement she heard her voice, light and careless, answering Naomi's question.

'Yes, that's him,' she agreed. 'How amazing. I really had no idea that I was mixing with the rich and famous.'

'Do you want to keep the magazine as a souvenir?' asked Naomi.

Kate looked at it as if she had been offered a tarantula. Then she rose to her feet and strode across the terrace, conscious only of an urgent need to escape before she burst into tears.

'No, you keep it,' she said in a muffled voice. 'After all, Philip Andronikos means nothing to me and I'll be moving on pretty soon. I want to travel as light as I can.'

As she neared the door of the house she collided with the archaeology student Andrew Cameron, who was just descending from his ladder. His bony hands shot out to steady her, and his narrow freckled face creased into an expression of concern.

'Careful, Kate,' he urged. 'Hey, are you all right? You look awfully pale.'

'Just a slight headache,' lied Kate.

'Are you sure? Well, could you hold the ladder steady for me while I tie the next section of plastic down? If we get another downpour like we had last week the pottery will be soaked.'

'All right,' agreed Kate.

She was gripping the rickety metal ladder firmly when Andrew suddenly gave a low whistle.

'There's another poor fool who's taken a wrong turning,' he said, craning his long neck out from the edge of the grape arbour. 'You'd better go and flag him down, Katey. Tell him it's a cul de sac and he'd better turn around here while he can. Nice car, too.'

Kate opened the gate obediently and jogged down the path. Heading off unwary tourists who became lost in the maze of Nyssa's back alleys was all part of the day's work, and it was better than sitting around brooding. But, as she reached the bottom of the path and began to wave at the oncoming car, her legs suddenly turned to jelly. For there was something ominously familiar about that glossy white vehicle. Not to mention the man who was now climbing out of it. He stood still for a moment, tossing his car keys thoughtfully between cupped palms, and gazed at her with a hungry, appraising look. Then he strode along the rocky verge of the roadside and came to a halt in front of her. Reaching out his hand, he tidied a straggling auburn curl back from Kate's cheek and smiled down at her.

'So how's my wife?' he asked teasingly.

'Don't joke about it!'

Kate was surprised to hear the angry, ragged edge to her voice. Philip's eyebrows drew together in a frown.

'I thought you'd be pleased to see me,' he said reproachfully. 'Perhaps I'm wrong, but I thought there was a special closeness between us on Sunday night. Didn't you feel it too?'

Kate sensed hysteria mounting in herself. She clenched her hands so hard that the nails dug into her palms, and gave a short, brittle laugh.

'Yes, well, I believe that's quite common for disaster victims,' she said coolly. 'It's something to do with being thrown in at the deep end together, I suppose. But the disaster's over now, isn't it?'

'I see.'

His voice was suddenly cold and almost hostile. Instinctively Kate moved back a step, but with a swift movement he came towards her and seized her by the shoulders.

'What are you playing at, Katarina?' he asked softly.

She glanced up and saw a knot of interested watchers on the terrace. Naomi, Marion and Andrew. Too far away to hear what was said, but close enough to be avid onlookers.

'Philip,' she begged shakily, 'please don't make a scene about it. Yes, there was something special between us, but there's no future in it. You know that as well as I do.'

'Do I?' he demanded sardonically, tightening his grip on her shoulders. 'What do you think I came here for, then, Katarina?'

Out of the corner of her eye, she saw Andrew leave the group on the terrace and come loping down the path. Her throat constricted as she felt Philip's urgent fingers pressing into her flesh and saw his dark eyes blazing down at her with an unreadable expression.

'Oh, Philip, I don't know!' she exclaimed desperately.

'Don't you?' he insisted.

He looked down at her with an expression of such intense yearning that her bones seemed to melt inside her. For one insane moment she was tempted to fling herself into his arms, fiancée or no fiancée. But somehow she stayed calm enough to shake off his hold and step back. She looked at him out of cool green eyes and shook her head mutely.

'I came because I couldn't get you out of my mind,' said Philip urgently. 'There is something so fresh and lovely about you, Katarina. I hated to think I might never see you again. Can't we at least have dinner together and talk?'

Kate hardened her heart against the naked warmth in Philip's brown eyes and a slow rage began to mount inside her. How dared he say such things to her when he was engaged to another woman?

'No, Philip. There's no possible future in it,' she said curtly.

'Why not?'

She wanted to say 'Because you're marrying another woman', but the words stuck in her throat. She knew she would burst into tears if she uttered them. Then suddenly Andrew was beside her. Tall, brown-haired, good-natured Andrew, whom she had known since she was six years old. Andrew, who was like a second brother to her.

'Is everything all right, Katey?' he asked, laying a bony hand on her shoulder.

His gaze darted searchingly from Philip's angry, brooding face to her pale, distressed one. Then suddenly, to his astonishment, Kate put her arm firmly around his waist.

'Andrew, I was just explaining to Philip that I can't have dinner with him because you're my boyfriend,' she babbled nervously.

Andrew caught the imploring note in her voice and his arm tightened round her shoulder.

'Oh—er—yes, of course,' he said. 'Still, I appreciate all you've done for her, Mr Andronikos. My name's Cameron, by the way. Andrew Cameron. We were all worried sick about Kate when the earthquake hit. It was good of you to look after her so well.'

Andrew put out his hand. For an instant Philip regarded it with a hostile frown. Then, slowly and reluctantly, he put out his own. Kate felt an obscure pain as she watched the two men shake hands, overcome by a sudden vivid memory of Philip's deft fingers caressing her face and lifting her mouth to his. Frantically she broke into speech again.

'Yes, well, it was nice of you to call and see how I was getting on, Mr Andronikos, but, as you can see, I'm just fine,' she said hastily. 'So if there's nothing else . . .'

Her voice trailed away under the intent stare of those smouldering brown eyes.

'Oh, but there is something else, Miss Walsh,' rejoined Philip. 'I have a business proposition that I want to discuss with you.'

'Business proposition?' echoed Kate in bewilderment.

He inclined his head briefly, without ever taking his eyes off her face. She began to feel like a small bird trapped in the hypnotic gaze of a cobra. The word 'proposition' rang loudly in her head like the clang of a cash register.

'What kind of a proposition?' she asked nervously.

A gleam of amusement lit his angry features.

'I want you to take some photos for me. If you'd like to dine with me this evening I'll explain it all to you,' he promised.

Kate felt a pang of yearning, followed by an even sharper pang of apprehension. What sort of game was Philip Andronikos playing at? Did he see her as a gullible foreign tourist, who might be lured into a brief affair with him? Worse still, would he offer to set her up in a luxurious flat as his mistress? Was that how the jet-set behaved?

'I-I'm sorry,' she stammered breathlessly. 'I... I'm having dinner with Andy tonight.'

Philip shrugged indifferently.

'I'm sure Mr Cameron will excuse you for once,' he countered. 'Shall we say eight o'clock?'

He was already turning his back and striding down the hill, so that Kate had to run after him, her feet slipping and sliding in the tiny stones on the edge of the path.

'But I said no!' she exclaimed indignantly.

Philip turned back, his features composed into the resolute mask of a man used to getting his own way.

'Oh, but I won't take no for an answer,' he said softly. 'Mr Cameron, see that she comes tonight, won't you? I think she'll find the assignment congenial, and my terms are very generous.'

Ten seconds later he was behind the wheel of his gleaming white Saab, manoeuvring smoothly out of a tight corner and away down the road.

'Phew! What was all that about?' demanded Andrew, running his fingers through his shaggy brown hair.

'Don't ask!' retorted Kate savagely. 'Honestly, I could choke that man!'

Andrew grinned. 'That was obvious,' he agreed. 'Now how about explaining it all to an innocent bystander?'

'Oh, Andrew, you don't want to know!' groaned Kate. 'Anyway, I'm not going tonight. I'd rather have dinner with a Bengal tiger!'

'Hey, now wait a minute,' said Andrew in a puzzled voice. 'I don't understand this. I've known you since we were six years old, Kate. And, right from grade one, you always wanted to be a photographer. Even when your family gave you all that flak about getting a steady job, you still stuck to your guns and did what you wanted. Now a chance comes up which might be the biggest break you're ever likely to get and you're telling me you won't take it? Why the hell not?'

Kate twisted her hands together and shrugged.

'I can't explain,' she said miserably.

'Is it because you don't think your work will be good enough?' asked Andrew.

Kate swallowed, feeling her throat tighten.

'Not exactly,' she said despairingly. 'Although it probably won't.'

Andrew seized her by the shoulders.

'Kate, you've got to stop this nonsense,' he urged. 'You're always putting yourself down. I know it's because your family always made you feel that you were no good unless you became a lawyer and earned pots of money or at least got a steady job of some kind. But the truth is that you're terrific at what you do. You're a really talented photographer, but it's tough being a freelancer and you have to take every opportunity you get. So, if you're worrying that this Andronikos chap won't like your photos, then take it from me: he'll love them.'

'It's not really that,' admitted Kate with a ragged sigh. 'It's something...a bit more personal.'

'Did he make a pass at you the night of the earthquake?' demanded Andrew.

'Not exactly,' replied Kate. 'But I'm afraid he might try it on tonight. And he's engaged to somebody else, Andy!'

'Oh, for heaven's sake!' cried Andrew. 'Of all the pathetic excuses! If he didn't have his wicked way with you when you were alone on a mountainside you ought to be pretty safe in a restaurant surrounded by dozens of other people. Now come on, Katey, pull yourself together and get ready. You're going!'

'You really think I should?' asked Kate uncertainly.

'Of course you should. You'd be mad if you didn't!'

'I suppose you're right,' admitted Kate reluctantly. 'Well, the only question now is what do I wear?'

By the time Philip arrived at eight o'clock Kate was as well-dressed as her limited resources allowed. Feminine to the core, she did not want to appear in the same jade-green skirt and blouse that she had worn on the evening of the earthquake. Even if she had no intention of allowing Philip Andronikos to seduce her, she wanted him to realise what he was missing out on. Feeling that the honour of the dig was at stake, the other women rallied around to produce a very presentable outfit. Not an easy task in a place where formal dress meant jeans without paint-stains and an army shirt without holes! But somehow they achieved it. Dark-haired Naomi, who was as slim as Kate, produced a cherry-red cocktail dress with a frilled hem and a low-cut neckline. Charlotte contributed an opal pendant on a gold chain, Marion combed up her hair and Silvana did her make-up. When at last Philip's firm, confident knock sounded at the front door Kate was sure she looked her best. Yet somehow her heart was beating a frenzied tattoo as she unlocked the heavy front door.

'Hello,' she said huskily.

Philip was silent for a moment, staring back at her with an elusive smile playing around his lips. Although he wore an impeccably tailored dinner suit, she was still conscious of a hint of wildness about him. Somehow the powerful shoulders seemed to strain against the dark fabric of his jacket, while his alert, watchful stance suggested the grace of a jungle cat. He might be masquerading as a conventional businessman, thought Kate with a tremor of excitement, but underneath he's completely primitive. The kind of man who will do and say whatever he likes.

'I've missed you,' said Philip frankly.

Kate flushed.

'Since this afternoon?' she demanded with deliberate lightness.

'No. Since we spent the night together,' he replied.

'Philip, please don't!' she begged.

'As you wish, Katarina. But sooner or later we will have to discuss it. Is this your shawl on the hall-stand? I thought we'd eat at Porto Carras, if that suits you.'

'Yes, of course,' said Kate stiffly.

Porto Carras was a luxury tourist complex on the west side of the Sithoniá peninsula. Kate had driven past it on several occasions, but had never expected to set foot inside it. In other circumstances she would have enjoyed the drive to Porto Carras. It was a fine, cool night, and the moon was spilling its milky radiance across the dark waters of the Kólpos Kassándras. But, after their opening skirmish, Philip Andronikos seemed to feel no need to engage in meaningless small talk, and Kate's few attempts at conversation soon petered out. On the whole it was a relief when the journey came to an end and they saw the lights of the luxury hotel at Porto Carras loom out of the darkness on their left.

'It looks like an ocean liner, doesn't it?' commented Kate.

'Exactly,' agreed Philip. 'Even more so in the daylight with that enormous superstructure. Personally I prefer the lower, more traditional style of Greek building. But the concept behind this place is excellent. It's not just a tourist complex, but a whole miniature economy for the people of this region. Vineyards, olive groves, fishing, you name it. And I think you'll find the restaurant and the views are excellent too.'

He was right on both counts. An impeccably groomed waiter showed them to a table overlooking the sea, and Kate gazed round her in awe. Huge gilt mirrors flanked the dining-room, the dance-floor had been polished till it shone like glass, the musicians were resplendent in traditional Greek costume and the table was a work of art. Candles flickered on either side of an arrangement of white iceberg roses, and their glowing light was reflected from crystal goblets, heavy silver cutlery and Wedgwood china. And, although they had an excellent view of the dance-floor, a screen of potted Kentia palms shielded them from the gaze of other diners. Philip seemed to accept all this luxury as his natural ambience, and he sat back in his chair with the air of a man who was completely at home.

'Well, what will you have to drink?' he asked.

Kate, still feeling overwhelmed, chose a safe gin and tonic, while Philip opted for ouzo, the traditional Greek aniseed liqueur. When the drinks arrived Philip raised his glass in a salute.

'*Yasu!*' he exclaimed.

'*Yasu!*' she replied.

'Now,' said Philip, setting down his glass after a swift gulp, 'perhaps you will be good enough to explain why you are treating me as if I have bubonic plague.'

Kate choked on her drink, alarmed at such directness.

'I'm not!' she lied hastily, but the spreading colour in her cheeks betrayed her.

'Oh, yes, you are,' contradicted Philip. 'On Sunday night I had you in my arms, Katarina. Warm and soft and yielding. So soft and so yielding that I think I could have taken you without the slightest opposition.'

His dark eyes seemed to imprison her so that she sat trapped like a frightened bird in their penetrating stare. Her heart beat so wildly that she thought he must see it through the thin chiffon of her dress.

'That's not true!' she denied.

'Isn't it?' he demanded huskily. 'How strange. Do you know, I had the strongest impression on Sunday night that you longed for me to undress you and caress your naked flesh? That you wanted me to carry you to bed and take you, just as badly as I wanted to do it?'

'Stop it!' begged Kate, scarlet with embarrassment. 'People will hear you.'

'Oh, I think not,' said Philip mildly. 'I asked for a very private table precisely so that we could discuss all this without being overheard.'

'How dare you?' cried Kate through quivering lips. 'You told me you wanted to discuss business with me!'

'So I do,' agreed Philip with infuriating calm. 'But all in good time. First I want to know why your manner has changed so much towards me.'

'It hasn't,' said Kate with a toss of her flaming auburn curls.

'Hasn't it?' demanded Philip.

Suddenly his hand shot out, imprisoning hers. She looked down at the lean brown fingers that held her in a vice-like grip, at the sleek dark hair that covered Philip's powerful wrists beneath the crisp white cuffs. A little gasp escaped her.

'You're nothing but a savage underneath that expensive suit!' she accused angrily.

'Exactly,' agreed Philip, his eyes glittering dangerously. 'And smart women don't provoke savages. So why don't you finish your drink and then tell me why you have suddenly become so cold towards me?'

As he spoke his grip softened, till it was nothing more than a warm caress against her skin. Kate swallowed convulsively and tried to withdraw her hand.

'Give me one good reason why I should!' she flung at him.

His hand tightened again on her fingers.

'If I told you I fell half in love with you on Sunday night would that be good enough reason?' he demanded urgently.

It was all she could do to pull away from that warm, seductive hold. He's going to marry another woman, she told herself fiercely. This is nothing but a game to him. Tears prickled at the back of her eyelids. The haunting Remvetika music in the background, the soft lights, the scent of the roses were nothing but a snare that he had laid to trap her.

'No,' she retorted angrily.

'Katarina,' he begged, 'look at me. Say something to me.'

No power on earth could have stopped her from turning her head to face him. The tears brimmed over and sparkled on her lashes, but she held her head high and met his gaze.

'Why didn't you tell me you were engaged?' she whispered.

He sat back in his chair and a pained look came over his face.

'So that's it!' he said with a mirthless laugh. 'I might have known.'

'Yes, you might!' agreed Kate, stung beyond endurance. 'You might also refrain from telling other women you're half in love with them when you ought to be wholly in love with your fiancée!'

'My engagement has never been like that,' protested Philip. 'The match was arranged years ago by our families. Love has nothing to do with it!'

'Really?' demanded Kate furiously. 'Then you have my sympathy, but I still don't see that you have any right to go around making love to other women.'

'I see!' retorted Philip with equal fury. 'You're absolutely right, of course. Obviously I should have taken the precaution of breaking off my engagement before I set out on my journey last weekend!'

'I didn't say that!' hissed Kate. 'But you certainly should have taken the precaution of keeping your hands off me. What possible right do you have to lead me into some squalid little affair that I can only regret?'

Philip leant across the table, his eyes flashing, ready to reply. But at that moment a waiter arrived, coughed discreetly and produced two large leather-clad menus. Kate's hands trembled as she took the menu which the waiter opened ceremoniously in front of her. She felt that at last she was beginning to get her bearings with Philip Andronikos, but she didn't like the direction the conversation was taking at all. Obviously the time she had spent in his arms at Ayía Sofía, which had seemed so precious and magical to her, meant absolutely nothing to him. Even if the emotion that had flared up between them really was love, what difference did it make? Hadn't he just said that love had nothing to do with marriage? What she must do was stay calm and distant and remember that she was only here for the sake of her career. Grimly she scanned the menu.

'Do you really hate our Greek cuisine so much that it makes you scowl like that?' asked Philip mockingly.

Kate started.

'No, of course not!' she replied in an embarrassed tone. 'I love Greek food. It's just that it's all so unfamiliar.'

'Then perhaps you will allow me to help you choose. Let me explain what all this means.'

Philip led her step by step through the menu, and Kate ordered mesethakia, a mixed hors d'oeuvre with pickled olives, cheese and squid, followed by spit-roasted lamb with potatoes and a side-dish of stuffed peppers. Once the waiter had taken their orders she sat back in her chair with her hands clenched tightly in her lap and her gaze fixed stonily on a point six inches above Philip's head.

'Look at me, damn you,' said Philip.

Her eyes darted angrily down to meet his, then slewed away. He gave a harsh laugh.

'You're wrong about one thing, you know,' he said meditatively.

'Oh. What's that?' demanded Kate frostily.

'I never intended to lead you into a squalid little affair that you'd regret.'

'Is that right? And just what exactly did you intend?' she parried.

'Nothing specific!' he retorted irritably. 'For heaven's sake, woman! Do you think I set the whole thing up? You must have an amazing view of my talents if you think I can turn on an earthquake purely in order to lure you into my bed!'

Kate's lips twitched unwillingly.

'I wouldn't put it past you!' she said in a stormy voice.

'And while you're busy blackening my character please remember that I had you in my bed and didn't lay a finger on you.'

'That's true,' admitted Kate.

Philip looked at her with an intent searching gaze that seemed to strip her naked. Then his fingers came out and touched her gently under the chin.

'So can't you accept that I was carried away when I kissed you, just as you were?' he asked.

Kate swallowed, acutely conscious of his feather-like touch. Reaching up her own hand, she moved his fingers away.

'Even if you were, then where does that leave us?' she retorted bitterly. 'All right, so we felt a mutual attraction, but there's no future in it, is there?'

Philip's eyes blazed defiantly.

'I'm not so sure about that,' he murmured.

'What do you mean?' demanded Kate with an edge of panic in her voice. 'What do you want from me, Philip?'

At that moment the waiter arrived with a bottle of the ruby-red Mavrodafni wine for which the area was famous. There was a brief pause as Philip sniffed the powerful fruity bouquet and then swirled the wine thoughtfully on his palate. With a satisfied nod he motioned for their glasses to be filled. Only when the waiter had withdrawn did he answer Kate's question.

'I don't know what I want from you,' he confessed moodily. 'Everything. Nothing. If you're asking me whether I want to take you to bed, well of course I do! You're all woman, Katarina. Beautiful, sensual, yielding. I want to crush you against me and feel you throbbing with longing beneath me. I want to make you ache with need for me.'

Kate felt an unwilling thrill of excitement at his words.

'Don't, Philip,' she protested. 'You mustn't say these things! You're already committed to somebody else.'

Philip gritted his teeth.

'Committed!' he said. 'It sounds like a prisoner, doesn't it? Committed for trial, committed to gaol. And that's what it feels like sometimes. Do you have any idea what an arranged match is actually like, Katarina?'

'No,' admitted Kate.

'Well, let me tell you,' said Philip in a low, urgent voice. 'Let me just tell you how I came to be engaged to Irene. I wasn't always wealthy, you know. In fact, I was poor—dirt poor. I didn't even own my first pair of shoes until I was fifteen years old, but right from the start I was ambitious. When I was seventeen years old I went to London and started working twenty hours a day in a hotel, trying to get enough money together to start up my own business. After I came back to Greece three years later I found a run-down tavern in Sithoniá, and I pestered everyone I knew for help. Most people

laughed at my ambitions, but Irene's father Con lent me
money, and my own father sank every last drachma he
had into the business. I won't bore you with the details,
but within two years the place was showing a good profit.
At that point Con approached my father and suggested
a match between their children to cement the part-
nership. I was twenty-two then. Irene was seven.'

'Seven!' echoed Kate in an appalled voice. 'That's
awful!'

Philip shrugged.

'It was the custom,' he said. 'And it suited everybody
well enough at the time. For me it was a chance to
postpone any family obligations well into the future,
which meant I could throw myself into my work. And
Irene was able to rule the roost among the other seven-
year-olds by bragging about the wealthy husband she was
going to have.'

Kate choked on an unwilling laugh.

'It sounds barbarous,' she said, shaking her head.

'I don't think I realised how barbarous it was at the
time,' agreed Philip seriously. 'But, in all fairness, I must
say that such marriages often work out very well. Frequently the partners do come to love each other.'

Kate felt her palms grow damp and there was a sensation of tightness in her chest, but she had to put the
question that was preying on her mind.

'Do you love Irene?' she asked haltingly.

A pained expression came over Philip's face. For the
first time Kate noticed the lines of anxiety or weariness
etched from his nose to the corners of his mouth.

'No,' he replied curtly. 'At first I was so busy that I
hardly saw her. And then later, as the hotel chain grew
bigger and more money came in, she was sent away to
boarding-school in England. After that she went to a
Swiss finishing-school. It's only this year that I've had
much to do with her.'

Something in his tone roused Kate to a profound sense of uneasiness.

'Don't...don't you get along well together?' she asked.

Philip picked up his glass and took an impatient gulp.

'She's a spoilt brat,' he said bluntly. 'Not that it's entirely her fault. Her mother was a very foolish woman, and finding herself suddenly wealthy went to her head. She brought up Irene and her brother Stavros to be as frivolous and extravagant as she is herself. No, I don't get along well with Irene. As a matter of fact, I'd really begun to believe that I'd lost all capacity for feeling. Until I met you.'

'Don't, Philip!' begged Kate. 'It's impossible!'

'Is it?' demanded Philip. 'Perhaps things are only impossible if we make them so!'

He took her hand and felt it fluttering nervously under his fingers.

'Didn't you tell me,' he murmured softly, 'that sometimes you have to take rash moves if you don't want to settle for second best in your life?'

She was silent, staring at him with wide green eyes.

'I'm about to take a very rash move,' said Philip. 'I want to ask you something.'

Deep down she knew she should make him stop, but she could not find the will-power to do so.

'What is it?' she whispered.

'Come away with me on my yacht,' he urged. 'Just for a few days. All I want is a chance to get to know you, Katarina. It's as simple and difficult as that.'

'No!' she cried, dragging her hand out of his. 'It's impossible, Philip. Anyway, I thought you disapproved of foreigners who made love with men they hardly knew!'

'I do. But there is no need for any lovemaking. We could simply enjoy the cruise together, go fishing, visit some of the islands, spend time talking. I feel we have a lot to say to each other, don't you?'

Kate paused, reluctantly tempted. How she would love to sail out into the sparkling blue waters of the Aegean with Philip beside her! But the idea was outrageous.

'No!' she said desperately. 'Perhaps things would be different if you weren't engaged to Irene, but you are!'

He laughed derisively.

'And so I have to break my engagement before I can spend any time alone with you?' he demanded. 'You ask a lot for a single date, Katarina.'

'I can't help that,' retorted Kate doggedly. 'It just seems like a matter of simple decency to me.'

'Decency?' echoed Philip in a baffled voice. 'You hitch-hike around Europe alone, and yet you talk to me of decency? Are you serious, or is this some game you are playing with me?'

His liquid dark eyes met hers with a mixture of scepticism, amusement and growing interest. Kate gritted her teeth in exasperation. Suddenly the whole situation became horribly clear to her. In Philip's view a girl who could hitch around Europe on her own obviously had no moral scruples of any kind. So he was hardly likely to believe that Kate was genuinely troubled by the thought of having a fling with somebody else's fiancée. She searched desperately for an argument that would mean something to him.

'Yes, I am serious!' she said, tossing her head so that her auburn curls blazed in the candlelight. 'Just because I travel alone doesn't mean that I'm easy game for a man who wants a cheap sexual adventure. I can't come on a cruise with you, and I am offended that you should even suggest it. How could I go with you? It would be... it would be a stain upon my honour!'

There! she thought triumphantly. That should be Greek enough to convince him that I mean what I'm saying. But it did more than simply convince Philip. A look of consternation passed over his face.

'I have offended you!' he said. 'I apologise, Katarina. The truth is that I misjudged you when I first met you.'

'What do you mean?' asked Kate cautiously.

Philip fixed her with a gaze that seemed to scorch right through her thin chiffon dress.

'Simply this,' he admitted huskily. 'When I found you alone and unprotected on the mountainside I thought you did not care about your honour. But now I see that I was wrong. In fact, your honour is so important to you that you will not even spend time alone with a man, much less offer him the gift of your body. That pleases me. It pleases me very much indeed. I never expected to find a foreign girl of your age who was still a virgin.'

Kate's face flamed. A virgin! she thought with a sudden vivid recollection of her torrid affair with Leon Clark. Well, that was over and done with, and it was hardly any of Philip's business anyway. And there was certainly no point in mentioning it now. So she simply murmured something inaudible, lowered her eyes and fingered a white rose in the vase in front of her. Philip gazed at her with an expression of warm approval in his dark eyes.

'So you are keeping yourself for one man alone?' he mused. 'I envy him, Katarina. Does he know what a prize he has found in you?'

'Who?' replied Kate blankly.

'Your boyfriend,' prompted Philip impatiently.

'Boyfriend?' echoed Kate in a puzzled voice. She had forgotten all about Andrew. Then memory dawned. But suddenly she felt ashamed of her impulsive lie. Whatever he had left unsaid at their first meeting, Philip had been totally honest with her tonight. Didn't she owe him the same frankness?

'Andrew's not really my boyfriend,' she admitted reluctantly. 'Although he is my very dear friend. We were next-door neighbours in a country town in New South Wales, and you can't get much closer than that. So naturally, when I decided to come to Europe, I wanted to visit him at Nyssa. But there's no romance between us. I only said that to try and fend you off. I'm sorry for deceiving you.'

But to her surprise Philip showed no sign of resentment.

'You lied for the best possible reason,' he conceded magnanimously. 'So how can I blame you for it? Besides, I cannot help feeling pleased to learn that you are not planning to marry that undoubtedly very ordinary young man. Yet does romance play no part in your life at all?'

'I didn't say that,' retorted Kate a shade too quickly. She thought of Leon and a shadow passed over her face. 'Love is just as important to me as to any other woman, but I can't regard it as a business arrangement the way you Greeks seem to. Or as a game.'

'Whereas I have never seen it as anything but a business or a game,' sighed Philip, sipping his wine. 'One marries a wife with a dowry, one plays games with divorcees who want a good time, but what does one do with a girl like you, Katarina? A girl who only wants love? Love! An impossible ambition, but one that is beginning to intrigue me, I must confess.'

His voice was rich and soft and velvety, and his dark eyes held hers as if he had some hypnotic power over her. For an instant Kate trembled, feeling a crazy impulse to change her mind about the cruise even now. She shivered and picked up her glass, breaking the spell.

'One discusses business with her,' she said firmly. 'Real business, not dowries. Insurance photos, travel brochures, that sort of thing.'

Philip's gaze rested hungrily on her features.

'Is that your last word on the subject?' he demanded.

'Yes!' said Kate fervently.

With a great effort of will, she picked up her bag and stared unwaveringly at Philip.

'The only relationship I'm prepared to have with you is a business one,' she insisted. 'So either we talk business from now on or I'm leaving.'

'Very well, then,' agreed Philip with a sigh. 'To business. I'm opening a new hotel at Áyios Dimitrios on the east side of the Sithoniá peninsula next month. It's called Hotel Ariadne and it's not unlike this place in many ways. Oh, not the architecture—I've gone for a cluster of low traditional buildings around a central entertainment centre—but the total package. It's part of a complex of activities designed to provide the local people with year-round employment. Potteries, textiles, olive processing, vineyards. This project represents the dream of a lifetime come true for me. I grew up in Áyios Dimitrios when the villagers had nothing but glorious scenery and abject poverty. What I want to create is not just seasonal employment, but a total economic package for them, so that they will have secure work all year round and a real hope for their children's future. It's costing me a fortune, but it will be worth every drachma. Most of the photographic work for publicity was done earlier in the year, but I'm thinking of setting up some special off-season tours and I want someone to do the brochures for them. I'll also need a few photos taken of my yacht for insurance purposes. I thought you might be interested. There's a fully equipped dark-room at the hotel, or you could send your photos to Thessaloníki for processing.'

Kate's bag slipped unnoticed to the floor and her eyes shone.

'B-but why me?' she stammered. 'I'm not well known or anything.'

Philip shrugged.

'No, but you're talented,' he said. 'If you think I'm doing this because I'm trying to seduce you, then think again. I never do business on that basis. It's only hack work, of course, but it will give you enough money to keep doing the sort of photos you really want to do. Like those *Windmills of Mykonos* prints you showed me at Ayía Sofía. Now, you'll want to know the terms of our arrangement. I'll need all the photos completed and ready to go four weeks from today. You can stay at one of the villas at the Ariadne while you're working. And I'd pay you...'

He named a sum that made Kate gasp.

'I can't believe it,' she said. 'I'll be able to live on that for a year, while I take the kind of photos that I like. Landscapes, people, compositions of light and shade. I'll even be able to afford a decent telephoto lens.'

Philip looked amused.

'There speaks an artist,' he murmured. 'Well, will you take the job?'

'Yes,' she said breathlessly. 'When do you want me to start?'

'Tomorrow, preferably. Does that suit you?'

'Yes,' agreed Kate, feeling slightly dazed at the speed with which events were happening. 'I've finished the work I was doing at the dig, so that's no problem. I'll catch the first bus I can get.'

'There's no need for that,' cut in Philip. 'I'll come and fetch you. But there is one point I wish to emphasise to you.'

'Yes?' said Kate.

'It is this: I value my privacy, and under no circumstances do I want it invaded. There are certain people in the media who will pay handsomely for information about the rich and famous. I do not want to find my taste in wine, women, automobiles or anything else a subject for speculation in the gutter Press. Anyone who sells such information about me will suffer for it. Do I make myself clear?'

There was no doubting Philip's sincerity. His dark eyes blazed and his lean, powerful hands were clenched on the tablecloth.

'I wouldn't think of doing such a thing!' exclaimed Kate indignantly.

Some of the tension went out of Philip's face. A wry smile lurked suddenly around the corners of his mouth.

'Good,' he said. 'Then let's finish our meal.'

The next two hours slipped by in a daze for Kate. Philip was the perfect host, chatting amiably about the sights of the Halkidiki, urging her to try various delicacies from the menu, leading her out on to the dance-floor. And yet the earlier intimacy between them had vanished completely. It was difficult to believe that Philip had ever told her he loved her or made his outrageous proposition to her. There was nothing of the lover about him now. Instead he was every inch the suave and ruthless businessman in total control of the situation.

Yet, as Philip handed her into the car, he paused for a moment with his hand on her elbow.

'By the way, Katarina,' he said coolly, 'if you ever change your mind my earlier offer about the cruise still stands.'

CHAPTER THREE

KATE woke early the next morning and spent twenty minutes feverishly packing her bags and checking her cameras. Although it was not yet dawn, the house was already full of activity as the archaeological team brewed coffee over a gas stove and loaded the donkeys with sieves and picks and drawing equipment for the day's digging.

'Now remember, you can always come back here if things don't work out at Áyios Dimitrios,' said Charlotte, folding her in a swift hug. 'We'll be digging here till the end of October, and you know you're always welcome.'

'Thanks, Charlie,' replied Kate gratefully. 'If anything goes wrong I'll remember that.'

She watched them all until they vanished out of sight in the thick scrub behind the village. Andrew turned and gave her a final wave, and for a couple of minutes she could hear the sound of their voices and the occasional hoarse bray of a donkey; then even that ceased. She was left alone on the terrace in the pearly grey light, fiddling nervously with the strap on her camera bag and wondering what the future held for her. Then the sun rose blood-red in the east, lighting up the dark blue saw-toothed peaks of Mount Athos across the gulf. A moment later the sound of an expensive car engine came purring up from the village. Kate felt her pulses race tumultuously as she saw the familiar glossy white car rounding the final bend near the villa, sending the hens scattering to each side. Snatching up her bags, she hurried down the path and waited by the roadside, only to stop dead with an unreasonable sense of disappointment. For it was not Philip Andronikos who stepped out of the car, but a chauffeur in a grey uniform.

'Good morning, ma'am. My name is Yannis Lemnos. Are you Miss Walsh?'

'Yes,' said Kate.

'Mr Andronikos sent me to fetch you. He was too busy to come himself.'

Of course, thought Kate with an irrational twinge of disappointment. I told him I only wanted a business relationship with him and he's obviously accepted that. I probably won't even see him while I'm working at Áyios Dimitrios. Just as well, really.

She tried to keep her mind on the scenery as they drove up the coast of the Sithoniá peninsula. It was certainly a beautiful place with its craggy hills cloaked in drab green holly oak and arbutus scrub, splashed here and there with patches of purple heather. The road swooped and soared like a roller-coaster, opening up new vistas of pine-clad hillsides, gleaming sand and azure sea. Here and there were roadside shrines, and high on the slopes above the road shaggy long-eared goats browsed among the bushes. Once or twice they passed through white-washed villages, where donkeys laden with firewood trotted hastily out of their way, but most of the time there was nothing but the wild landscape and the blue sea. After about an hour's drive, Yannis turned off the road into a thick pine forest.

'Here we are,' he said. 'Áyios Dimitrios is just over the next hill. Or at least the hotel complex is. The original village is half a kilometre away.'

'Oh, how pretty!' exclaimed Kate, as the car breasted the rise. 'But this must be the original village, surely?'

'No,' said Yannis, smiling and shaking his head. 'Mr Andronikos likes everything old-fashioned, so he had it built this way, but it's all new really.'

He brought the car to a halt in the middle of what seemed at first sight to be a traditional Greek village. Except that no Greek village had ever been quite so beautiful. Around a central square were grouped half a dozen two-storey whitewashed buildings. The square itself was paved with terracotta tiles, laid in a herringbone pattern around a central fountain which cascaded musically around the feet of a bronze statue. Shady peppercorn trees rustled softly in the breeze, and white tables and chairs with big striped umbrellas sat invitingly amid urns full of geraniums. Through an archway to one side of the square, Kate caught an inviting glimpse of a tiled swimming-pool. As a backdrop to the whole scene there was the intense dark blue water of the Mediterranean sea, sparkling vividly in the sun.

Kate was still standing enraptured when a door opened in the building beside her. She half turned, catching a glimpse of the sign that said 'Reception' and smiled hesitantly, assuming that it was one of the hotel employees coming to greet her. But the man who came striding across the square to meet her was Philip Andronikos himself.

Her breath caught in her throat as she saw that lean, powerful figure prowling towards her. He was dressed very simply in navy blue linen shorts, a striped opennecked top and rope-soled shoes, but there was no mistaking the air of assurance that clung to him. Perhaps he was only frowning because of the glare of the sun, but Kate felt that his narrowed eyes were stripping her bare and appraising her. A tremor of alarm went through her as she realised that this scrutiny did not dismay her as it should. In fact, a tiny shudder of pleasure went through her as his gaze rested on her body.

'So you came, then?' he said softly.

'As you see.'

Her eyes met his directly. For a moment they both stood motionless, and Kate saw a hungry longing in his face. All thoughts of Irene Marmara vanished from her head. If they had been alone pure madness might have made her put out her arms to him. She might even have reached up a hesitant finger and touched the muscle that twitched in his cheek. But they were not alone. Yannis was standing by the boot of the car, holding her bags and looking expectantly at Philip.

'Take those along to Miss Walsh's villa, Yannis,' instructed Philip. 'Have you had breakfast, Miss Walsh?'

'Yes, thank you.'

'Then I'll show you around and you can start work as soon as you're ready.'

They followed Yannis up a pathway of rammed earth that wound between the trees. The air was full of the scent of pine needles, and Kate sniffed delightedly.

'This is the most amazing place,' she murmured. 'From the road it looks just like an unspoilt wilderness. You'd never guess there was a hotel here.'

'Well, that was my intention,' said Philip. 'It remains to be seen whether people will like it or not. Now we'll just leave your bags in your villa and then we'll do the grand tour of the place.'

Kate had a swift impression of red geraniums, pale blue shutters and a luxurious suite of rooms, then Philip had deposited her bags and was ushering her back along the path. The grand tour was certainly impressive. Hotel Ariadne, Áyios Dimitrios had not won its 'luxury class' rating for nothing. In addition to sumptuous accommodation, a ballroom, five swimming-pools, tennis courts, a nine-hole golf course, marina facilities and a children's playground, it boasted magnificent views and beautifully landscaped surroundings. Yet the part that Kate really enjoyed most was the visit to the original village of Áyios Dimitrios, where Philip was greeted like a folk hero and wrinkled old ladies in black dresses offered them coffee and ouzo.

As they left the village a sudden bend in the path led them out into a clearing on a hillside overlooking the sea. Kate caught her breath at the rugged grandeur of the view that opened out before her. Down below, the cobalt-blue waters of the Kolpos Agiou Orous spread out in a gleaming panorama right across to the peninsula on the other side.

'It's magnificent!' exclaimed Kate. 'I can't wait to begin taking photos.'

Philip gazed down at the bay with a thoughtful expression.

'Well, if you really mean that you can start right away,' he said. 'I've got a subject for you down there.'

'Do you mean the view?' asked Kate, shading her eyes against the glare.

'No. The motor yacht about four hundred metres out. See it? No, more to your left.'

Suddenly his hands seized her shoulders. For one heart-stopping moment she felt his warm hold through her thin cotton shirt and allowed herself to enjoy the closeness of his body behind her. She was acutely aware of the strength in his lean brown arms, of the faint spicy odour of his cologne, of the overpowering animal magnetism of the man. Then he turned her several degrees to the left, pointed down at the bay and spoke in a brisk, impersonal voice.

'Over there. See?'

'Oh, yes! Goodness, it's huge, isn't it?'

'Forty-six metres of pure luxury,' said Philip with satisfaction. 'It's called the *Eleftheria* and I intend to let it out for charters next summer. I've had it extensively refitted, and I need good-quality photos for the insurance company. So the sooner you can get to work, the better.'

'Whenever you like,' agreed Kate eagerly.

Half an hour later they were climbing aboard the *Eleftheria*. Philip brought the speedboat effortlessly up to the gleaming white yacht and cut the motor at exactly the right moment so that they drifted alongside with only the faintest bump. A smiling young steward, dressed in a white uniform with a great deal of gold braid, was waiting at the top of the ladder to help them aboard. As Kate handed him her travel-stained camera bag and leapt lightly on to the deck she felt suddenly conscious of her own shabbiness. Even the pretty lace-trimmed blouse and floral shorts, which she had bought in the street-market at Thessaloníki only a week before, suddenly seemed cheap and shoddy amid the opulence that now surrounded her. But Philip seemed to take the splendour of the vessel entirely for granted.

'Good morning, Laki,' he remarked pleasantly. 'This is Miss Walsh. She's come to take some photos of the yacht.'

'How do you do, ma'am?' said Laki, touching his peaked yachting cap.

'Are any of my guests on board at the moment?' asked Philip.

'No, sir. Monsieur Sauvignon, Mr Stavros and Miss Irene have all gone spearfishing.'

Kate felt an unpleasant jolt of shock at this statement. Miss Irene? Did he mean Irene Marmara, Philip's fiancée? She eyed Philip searchingly, half expecting to see his face light up at the mention of the name. But Philip was frowning in a preoccupied fashion.

'Were they alone?' he asked sharply.

'No, sir. Giorgos went with them. You gave orders——'

'Yes, yes. Very well,' replied Philip impatiently, 'we'll see them at lunchtime, then. Come along, Katarina, and I'll show you round the yacht.'

Kate followed Philip along the shiny, varnished surface of the deck with a strong sense of uneasiness. Her stomach seemed to be fluttering as nervously as if she were standing on the edge of a cliff, and the thought of lunching with the unknown Irene filled her with apprehension. She doesn't need to know that I spent the night with Philip, she told herself fiercely. Or that he kissed me. And, anyway, it's only going to be a business relationship from now on.

'I'll show you the living quarters first,' said Philip, cutting into her troubled thoughts. 'I've had the saloon redone to my own taste, and I'll need photos of all the fittings.'

Kate forgot her troubles and gave a little gasp of delight as he flicked a switch, lighting up an interior which would have graced a drawing-room in even the most luxurious of modern apartments. Leather ceilings, lacquered sycamore walls and handwoven Greek carpets combined to produce an atmosphere of understated elegance. Cream leather loungers strewn with autumn-toned scatter cushions lined the walls, a sycamore coffee-table was bolted to the floor, expensive paintings hung on the walls and an overhead film projector promised the best of entertainment. Philip let her take her time admiring every feature of the place before leading her through a sliding glass door into the dining-room.

'How do you like it?' he asked with a touch of pride.

'I—it's superb!' exclaimed Kate, staring open-mouthed at the back-lit drop-ceiling inset with mirrors, the sycamore and laminate dining table, the cream leather chairs and the huge aquarium, which dominated one wall.

'We'll just have a quick look at the guest suites and then I'll take you through to my office,' promised Philip. 'Nikos, my private secretary, is on board this morning, and he'll give you all the details of what the insurance company wants. Then you can start work whenever you like.'

There were five guest suites on the *Eleftheria*, each with its own bathroom, built-in wardrobe, complete entertainment system, consisting of television, hi-fi and video, and all the little touches that made life worth living: monogrammed towels and bathrobes, gold-plated taps, modern paintings to match the colour scheme and designer jewellery boxes to hold the rings and tiaras at the end of the day. Kate could not help wondering what might have happened if she had accepted Philip's invitation. She pictured herself cruising out to sea amid all this luxury. Days spent basking in the sun with the clear blue water of the Mediterranean lapping against the hull. Nights spent in Philip Andronikos's arms, shuddering with pleasure at the wanton caress of his strong brown hands on her naked skin . . .

'My private state-room is just up here, astern of the wheelhouse,' said Philip, climbing lithely up a companion-way and pausing at the top to offer Kate a hand. 'The bathroom in it can be blacked out fairly easily if you prefer to change your films in the dark, and, of course, you're welcome to leave your bag in here while you work.'

He flung open a door leading into a large cabin as elegantly furnished as any suite in the Hotel Ariadne. The velvety soft cream carpet deadened the sound of their footsteps, and white laminate cupboards contrasted with the luxuriant greenery of dozens of pot plants. An enormous bed dominated the centre of the room, and square portholes along one wall offered a dazzling sunlit view of the blue sea outside. Philip opened another door to display a bathroom lined with sycamore panelling and smoked glass, then led the way back to a table overlooking the water.

'Why don't you put your equipment here so that you can get sorted out?' he invited.

But Kate was scarcely listening. She had paused to look at a framed enlargement of a photograph which hung on one wall.

'Isn't that the hill village of Theológos on Thásos?' she demanded. 'I went there with Andrew a few weeks ago, and I think I've got a photo taken from exactly the same spot.'

She fished in a pocket of her camera bag for a small plastic wallet full of prints, and flicked through them.

'Yes, there it is!' she exclaimed delightedly, holding it up against the photo on the wall to compare the two.

'May I see?' asked Philip.

'Yes, of course.'

She handed him the wallet and sat down at the table to begin assembling her equipment. Philip's face took on an intent, absorbed expression as he compared the two prints.

'Yours is by far the better photo,' he said thoughtfully. 'How interesting! As you say, they are taken from almost exactly the same spot and yet your picture captures the haunting, romantic quality of the village in the way the other does not. May I look at the rest of these?'

'Mmm. Be my guest,' agreed Kate in a preoccupied voice, hunting through the pockets of her bag for a filter. 'There's nothing very exciting among them, though. They were mostly character studies of people that I saw.'

Philip sat at the table and studied the photos. One of them, which was a study of an old man and woman trudging along a rough road together, seemed to catch his attention particularly and he turned back to it several times. And there was another photo of a young mother tossing her child playfully in the air in front of a dilapidated house that also caught his gaze.

'How much you are able to say without words, Katarina,' he said wonderingly. 'These two old people, for instance; you seem to be telling us that, no matter how rough the road, they will cope with the pitfalls because they are meeting them side by side. And this young woman with her laughing baby in front of that awful wreck of a house! Are you telling us perhaps that, however poor she may be, she is rich in the things that really matter and fortunate enough to realise it?'

Kate shrugged self-consciously.

'Yes, I suppose I was,' she agreed. 'I don't really stop to analyse it myself, but sometimes I'm profoundly moved by the sight of people doing quite ordinary things. Ordinary lives seem so rich to me sometimes, and I suspect we don't appreciate simple joys enough. At any rate, when I see something like that I try to capture the feeling it gives me on film.'

'And you succeed amazingly well,' Philip assured her. 'You know that you're remarkably talented, don't you?'

Kate wriggled uncomfortably.

'No, I'm not!' she protested. 'It's nice of you to say so, but it's not true. My parents always despaired of me because I wasn't good at anything, and that hasn't changed. I don't even seem to be good at finding the simple joys of life, let alone succeeding at anything. But I certainly admire the people who can.'

'What nonsense is this?' demanded Philip. 'You take photos of my countrymen that are so powerful that they move me almost to tears and you tell me you are no good at anything? And you make an evening in a run-down village like Ayía Sofía a memory I will treasure for the rest of my life and yet you say you have no talent for the simple joys? How can you be so blind to what you are, to the effect you have on other people? You should be living a full, rich life, glorying in your work and with a family who would love and appreciate your unique qualities.'

His hand came down on her shoulder and he gazed searchingly into her face, but she pulled away and took a couple of restless steps, twisting her hands together.

'Don't be ridiculous!' she said shakily. 'I'm not anything except a rather unsuccessful photographer. My parents were always high achievers, and I know I'm a disappointment to them. And who else is likely to love and appreciate my unique qualities, as you put it?'

Her whole body was tense with resentment and her voice sounded harsh with bitterness. Philip swung her round suddenly to face him and pulled her hard against his chest.

'I would!' he said fervently, burying his face in the heady fragrance of her hair. 'You're the kind of woman a man could worship for his entire life, Katarina. Full of character and love and warmth. This sarcasm doesn't suit you.'

For an instant Kate clung to him, intoxicated by the forbidden joy of his powerful arms around her, the caress of his lips on her hair, the sheer masculine magnetism that he radiated. Then she pushed him resolutely away.

'That's all very well,' she said in a taut, desperate voice. 'But you're already engaged to somebody else, and I didn't come here to be kissed, I came here to work! Now will you please leave me alone and let me get on with it?'

Philip's gaze lingered on her for a long, burning interval, as if he was committing her features to memory, then he turned abruptly towards the door.

'Yes, I suppose you're right,' he said curtly. 'Let me know if you need anything further. I'll be in the wheelhouse most of the time. And do join us for lunch in the dining-room at two o'clock, won't you?'

Left alone, Kate sat down at the table, buried her face in her hands and gave an inarticulate sob of dismay. If only Philip didn't have this devastating effect on her! She was drawn to him as inexorably as iron to a magnet, and when he held her in his arms it was easy to believe that he felt the same terrifying surge of emotion as she did. It was as if she had fallen into a river and was being carried along by a raging torrent of need and desire, but she mustn't allow herself to be dragged under. Philip was engaged to Irene and, whether he loved her or not, would no doubt marry her as custom demanded. Which left no place at all for Kate Walsh in his life. Except as a paid photographer. Giving herself a brisk shake, Kate rose to her feet and slung her camera determinedly over her shoulder. The sooner she finished these photos, the sooner she could leave the Hotel Ariadne. And that was undoubtedly the best thing for everyone concerned.

To her surprise the rest of the morning passed very quickly. Once she had her cameras and light meter set up, she became totally absorbed in the task of capturing the *Eleftheria* on film. It came as a shock when she heard the familiar sound of a speedboat motor approaching the yacht, and realised that it was after one-thirty. Leaping to her feet, she looked out of the window of the state-room. Bobbing alongside the yacht was a speedboat filled with a group of rowdy occupants. A white-uniformed crew-member in their midst seemed to be pleading with them to move out of his way and, as Kate watched transfixed, there was a sudden loud bump, followed by a scraping noise and a cry of dismay from the sailor. However, his passengers merely gave a raucous cheer before scrambling clumsily aboard. A sudden knock at the door made Kate swing sharply round. It was Philip's secretary, Nikos Vassiliou.

'Excuse me, Miss Walsh,' said Nikos apologetically, 'Miss Marmara and the others are back, so if you could come to the dining-room now I'd be grateful. She hates to be kept waiting at mealtimes.'

But when Kate made her way hesitantly into the dining-room she found it empty. Not knowing what to do, she hovered nervously, admiring the bright red and blue neon tetras in the aquarium. A white-clad steward materialised at her elbow and gave her a reassuring smile.

'Do sit down, Miss Walsh,' he urged. 'Mr Andronikos has just been called to the radio phone, but Miss Marmara and the others won't be long. Can I get you a drink while you're waiting?'

'Thank you,' replied Kate. 'I'll have a Perrier water, please.'

She was sipping hesitantly at her drink when a sudden commotion outside the dining-room announced the arrival of the others. To Kate's amazement a dark-haired girl, clad only in a skimpy red bikini, suddenly catapulted into the room, followed by a sun-bronzed young man, who was tickling her furiously. The girl shrieked and writhed protestingly, then suddenly froze as she caught sight of Kate. Her lustrous dark eyes had a vague, blurred look, and she put up one hand to her head and pushed back a strand of silky black hair.

'Who the hell are you?' she demanded peremptorily.

Awkwardly Kate rose to her feet and came around the table. Then she reached out her hand and smiled.

'My name is Kate Walsh,' she said. 'I'm a photographer. I've been doing some photos of the yacht for Mr Andronikos and he invited me to lunch.'

'Damn!' exclaimed the girl in the bikini. 'Isn't that the absolute limit?'

She ignored Kate's outstretched hand and looked around her for agreement. A second man, in his mid-twenties, dark-haired and handsome, had followed her into the room. The girl's voice rose in a penetrating whine.

'Stavros, Yves! I ask you! Isn't it too much? Every time Philip has some nobody on board to work for him he must always ask them to eat with us! I suppose it's because he came from the gutter himself that he only feels comfortable with servants. Next he'll be inviting the mechanics and the cleaners to sit down to meals with us. Well, I've had enough of it, do you hear me?'

She turned furiously to face Kate again, but almost lost her balance and had to clutch at one of the leather chairs for support.

'You can go and eat with the crew where you belong!' she spat.

Aghast at this outburst, Kate backed uneasily away, feeling that she would be only too happy to join the crew. But the dark-haired young man hurried forward and took her arm.

'Miss Walsh, please,' he begged. 'Wait! My sister doesn't mean a word of this. It is just that she has a touch of the sun. Come on, sit down, finish your drink.'

In a couple of swift, urgent movements he had coaxed Kate back into her seat and seized his sister none too gently by the arm. Giving her a reproving shake, he launched into a torrent of Greek, in which Kate could distinguish nothing more than the word 'Andronikos'. But whatever he said must have taken effect, for Irene allowed herself to be hauled unceremoniously into a chair. She sat there for a full minute, her eyes bright with unshed tears and her lower lip quivering like a child's, glaring at Kate. Then, as her brother gave her a sharp reminder in Greek, she capitulated.

'Please accept my apologies, Miss Walsh,' she muttered.

'Of course,' said Kate shakily, feeling that she would have liked the apologies much better if they had not been accompanied by such a venomous stare.

However, Irene's brother seemed perfectly satisfied with this conclusion. Seating himself at a place opposite Kate, he smiled charmingly around the table. Although Irene's lush curves were only held in place by the flimsiest of bikinis and Yves wore only brief shorts and a gold medallion, Stavros gave the impression that he was presiding over a formal luncheon party.

'Great, now we can all be friends and introduce ourselves,' he said in an accent that was more American than Greek. 'Miss Walsh, this is my sister, Irene Marmara, who is Philip Andronikos's fiancée. I'm Stavros Marmara, and this guy is our friend, Yves Sauvignon. Now what are we going to drink?'

Kate could not suppress the unwelcome suspicion that they had already had far too much to drink. Irene's face was flushed and perpsiring, and Yves was slurring his words slightly, while even Stavros seemed to have unnaturally bright eyes. They were just beginning a noisy argument on the rival merits of two different brands of French champagne when Philip appeared in the doorway. Kate gazed up with relief at the sight of that unsmiling face, and her noisy companions fell silent.

'Good afternoon,' said Philip smoothly. 'I apologise for keeping you all waiting. I'm surprised you didn't take the opportunity to get dressed, Irene.'

His glance flicked disapprovingly over the lush curves of her breasts in the revealing red bikini and came to a halt on Yves's arm, which was draped around her shoulder.

'Still, I'm sure we'll all be glad to wait while you go and slip into something more appropriate,' he finished.

'I wouldn't put you to the trouble,' sneered Irene. 'I'm perfectly happy as I am.'

'Oh, it's no trouble,' retorted Philip. 'In fact, I insist. Now run along, Irene.'

Kate caught her breath as she heard the steely undertone in his voice. For a moment she thought Irene would erupt like an angry child, but the younger girl simply thrust out her lip and flounced out of the room. When she returned five minutes later in a red and white striped Givenchy summer dress, Philip saluted her with his glass of Perrier water.

'You look very nice,' he said sincerely.

'Do I?' retorted Irene, slipping into her seat. 'Thanks for noticing!'

The tension between the pair made Kate feel thoroughly uncomfortable as the meal went on. She enjoyed the grilled octopus and the Greek salad, but there was no doubt that the conversation flagged. Stavros smiled warmly at her and tried to draw her into a discussion about skiing at Gstaad, but, since Kate had never skied, that proved a total failure. Seeing a wooden look on Philip's face, she realised to her astonishment that he was just as bored as she was by all the talk of slaloms and downhill runs. He made no attempt to join in the screams of laughter which accompanied Irene's anecdotes about the high life in Monaco and Biarritz and, when the steward reappeared with coffee and sticky pastries, he waved them away and pushed back his chair.

'Well, I've got work to do if you'll excuse me,' said Philip tersely. 'I'm planning on going ashore about four-thirty if that suits you, Katarina.'

'Yes, of course,' agreed Kate in a subdued voice. 'I think I'll get back to work too now. No, no coffee or pastry, thank you.'

She made her escape with relief, glad to be out of a gathering where she was so clearly not wanted. All the same, she could not help pondering on the nature of Philip's relationship with Irene as she went back to work. It was obvious that the shallow, pleasure-seeking life that Irene revelled in had little appeal for the man who was to marry her, and it was hard to see how the marriage could ever work. But it's nothing to do with me, Kate thought firmly. And if I encounter Irene again I'll just try and be as pleasant as I can towards her. Even so, she breathed more freely when she heard the run-about leave again at about three o'clock for another spearfishing excursion.

An hour or so later Kate was out on the lower deck of the yacht taking photos. Nikos had just come down to hand her the final page of the yacht's inventory when suddenly a loud noise rent the air. Kate shaded her eyes against the glare and saw the speedboat roaring across the water on its way back from the afternoon's spear-fishing. The secretary's eyes met hers in a shared moment of misgiving. Just as well Giorgos is with them, thought Kate. Not one of them is sober enough to handle a boat, let alone a spear-gun. Still, I don't suppose they can do much harm if they're properly supervised. But that was just where she was wrong.

'Look at them!' exclaimed Nikos in disgust. 'That stupid Yves will ram us if he's not careful. They're all as drunk as they can be!'

But at the last moment Yves cut the motor and drifted safely in to the side of the yacht. Irene gave a little whoop of triumph and swayed to her feet to congratulate him.

'I'd better go and give them a hand,' said Nikos, setting down his clipboard. 'She'll be lucky if she doesn't fall overboard in that condition.'

He went nimbly down the gangway and stood by as Giorgos made the speedboat fast. Yves rose to his feet with a spear-gun in his hand.

'Give that to me, sir,' said Nikos, eyeing it warily. 'Then you and Miss Marmara can come aboard.'

Yves held out the spear-gun, and at that moment everything seemed to happen at once. With a giggle Irene bent forward and tickled Yves, who doubled up with a startled cry. There was a loud whizzing thunk as the spear-gun discharged. Irene screamed piercingly, Nikos leapt back with an agonised howl and blood sprayed all over the foredeck.

Kate was down the companion-way in half a second flat to the spot where Nikos lay groaning horribly with a white-faced Giorgos bending over him.

'Stand aside,' she commanded. 'Let me look at him. Oh, no, it's an artery! We must stop the bleeding. Giorgos, clamp your hand over the wound.'

But Giorgos, with a low, strangled moan, simply swayed on his feet and fell down in a dead faint beside Nikos. Kate let out an impatient cry and pushed him aside. Careless of the blood that spurted over as she knelt beside Nikos, she grabbed his wounded forearm and held it firmly. Then, staggering to her feet, she began to drag him the short distance towards the speedboat.

'Quickly! We must get him to a doctor before he bleeds to death!' she panted.

Just at that moment Philip appeared at the top of the stairs and caught a swift glimpse of her swaying, blood-stained figure.

'Philip!' she cried. 'Help! Help!'

He was with her in an instant, his powerful arms flung round her, his frantic fingers exploring her face.

'Katarina! What happened to you? You're covered in blood!'

She saw his ashen face and realised that his concern for her. Desperately she tried to explain.

'No, no. It's not me! I'm all right! It's Nikos—the spear-gun. Oh, Philip, for heaven's sake, get him to a doctor!'

Somehow they succeeded in getting the injured man aboard and, while Kate kept the wound firmly clamped, Philip turned the speedboat towards the shore. Kate tried to blot out the sound of Nikos's agonised groans and Irene's hysterical sobbing, intent only on reaching a doctor. With a gasp of relief she saw the stone jetty looming up ahead of them.

There was a lot of frenzied shouting after that. Figures running with a stretcher, a man with a hypodermic syringe, calls for an ambulance. But Kate was no longer part of it. Pushing her hair back from her face with a shaky sigh, she realised suddenly that she was trembling all over and clad in nothing but a bloodstained blouse and shorts. A hot shower suddenly seemed like a very good idea.

When she reached her villa there was a chambermaid busy vacuuming her room. As she caught sight of Kate the girl made exactly the same mistake as Philip had done. With a little scream, she ran forward and clutched Kate's shoulders.

'Oh, miss, what happen? You have kill yourself!'

'No,' said Kate firmly, 'I'm fine. Somebody else was hurt, not me. It was Mr Andronikos's secretary, Nikos Vassiliou.'

The colour drained out of the girl's face.

'Nikos?' she exclaimed. 'Nikos is my brother. I am Anna Vassiliou. Is Nikos hurt bad?'

'I think he'll be all right. Why don't you go down and ask the doctor?'

'Oh, thank you, miss. I come back soon!'

Anna positively flew out of the room. With a sigh Kate made her way into the bathroom, stripped off her ruined clothes and stepped into the shower. After ten minutes under its warm rain, she felt restored enough to dry herself vigorously. A firm knock sounded in the other room and she glanced hastily around her. How silly! All her clean clothes were in the bedroom. Winding a towel around herself, she opened the door.

'Anna?' she asked.

But it wasn't Anna who stood there. It was Philip Andronikos. His eyes met hers with a naked warmth that made her unconsciously clutch the towel closer around her.

'I thought it was Anna,' she babbled in a high, un-natural voice that sounded quite unlike her own.

'I couldn't make you hear the front door with the shower running, so I just came in,' replied Philip, his gaze sliding down the slender column of her throat and coming to rest on the gentle swell of her bustline. 'I sent Anna away in the ambulance with Nikos.'

'How is Nikos?' asked Kate, lowering herself cautiously into an armchair and folding her arms nervously.

'Dr Papadopoulos is optimistic. According to him, you probably saved Nikos's life. Anyway, he's stopped the bleeding and put a drip in, and he says they'll do a blood transfusion in Thessaloníki. I won't know any more until I telephone the hospital tonight. But it's you I'm concerned about now.'

'Me?' demanded Kate, rising jerkily to her feet and pacing across the room. 'Why should you be concerned about me? I'm perfectly all right.'

She felt rather than heard him come after her; was suddenly acutely conscious of his warm, silent presence behind her. Then his hand seized her shoulder and he spun her round to face him. His breathing was fast and uneven and there was a pulse beating frantically in the side of his throat.

'When I saw you on the yacht covered in blood,' he said hoarsely, 'I died a thousand deaths. I was convinced you were going to die and I could only think what a fool I'd been never to do this.'

With ruthless force he dragged her into his arms and pressed his mouth down on hers. His kisses were deep and savage and demanding, and they released a hunger in her beyond anything she had ever imagined. A tiny groan escaped her as she opened her lips to his, then suddenly he had pulled her down on to the bed and they were rolling wildly in a frenzy of passion. The towel came loose and Philip flung it impatiently across the room before burying his head in the tender warmth of her breasts. His chin rasped her delicate flesh, sending shivers of excitement through her, then his tongue found the exquisite rosebud of her nipple. He went to work teasing and nibbling until she arched her back and thrust herself against him with a low moan of excitement. Her hands moved in frenzied circles across his back, pulling him hard against her so that they both quivered with longing. His lips moved up over her body in a trail of fire till they reached the slender column of her throat.

'Oh, I love you, Katarina!' he said thickly, burying his face in her hair.

She moaned indistinctly, pressing her body against his and shuddering with pleasure as his hands moved over her naked flesh. With a sudden cry of impatience Philip sprang to his feet and tore off his shirt.

'Philip, no!' cried Kate, sitting up sharply on the bed.

'Why not?' he demanded, his hands pausing on his belt-buckle. 'I want you, Katarina; I want you more than I've ever wanted any woman in my life. And you want me too, don't you?'

The throaty vibrance of his voice, the way he looked at her through narrowed eyes, the sheer animal grace of his stance sent a thrill of longing through Kate. But she reached out and dragged a corner of the bedspread up to cover herself.

'No,' she said faintly.

He laughed harshly and tore the flimsy covering out of her hands. His gaze rested deliberately on her taut pink nipples, the rapid rise and fall of her breasts, the pale curve of her hips.

'You're lying,' he whispered. His fingers caught in the silky tangle of her hair and he forced back her head so that she had to look at him. 'Aren't you, my love?'

She felt mesmerised by those blazing dark eyes, as if he could force any admission he liked from her. His mouth came down on hers, gently, teasingly, coaxing her into agreement. With one hand he reached out and lazily caressed the tips of her breasts, so that a quiver of need shot through her.

'Aren't you?' he insisted.

'Yes!' she cried in a tormented voice and struck his hand away from her.

Scrambling to her feet and dragging the bed cover after her like some preposterous sari, she crossed the room.

'All right, Philip,' she said in a low, angry voice. 'You can see perfectly well that I want you physically just as much as you want me. You've proved your point, so now you can just go away!'

'Is that what you think I'm doing?' demanded Philip furiously. 'Proving some stupid point?'

'Well, aren't you?' returned Kate angrily, picking up her travel bag and rummaging through it for something to wear.

'No!' said Philip through clenched teeth. 'Why the hell should I?'

Kate's fingers closed on a knit dress. Feverishly she hauled it over her head and ran her fingers through her tumbled hair. Then she tightened the belt and turned to face him.

'Because you men are all the same!' she retorted angrily. 'All you want is a quick grope to prove your manhood and then you'll be off like a shot!'

'Oh, I see,' said Philip sarcastically. 'You've had experience, have you?'

Kate hesitated, on the brink of spilling out all that had passed between her and Leon. It was tempting to blurt out the truth to Philip, to tell him of the horror she had felt when she'd learnt that the man who had seduced her was already married to another woman. But shame held her back.

'Not exactly,' she choked. 'But that doesn't mean that nobody has tried. And, let me tell you now, I'm just not interested in being a trophy on any man's wall. If you're trying to persuade me to have a cheap, nasty affair with you you can just forget it!'

To her horror she found that her legs were trembling. Kneeling down, she tried to zip up her bag, but her hands were shaking so much that she could not manage it. Suddenly she found that Philip was right behind her, his body warm and reassuring against her, his powerful fingers closing over hers.

'I do not want a cheap, nasty affair with you!' he said through his teeth.

'Don't you?' retorted Kate. 'Well, it certainly looks like it from where I am!'

Philip rose to his feet and paced around the room, rubbing his chin thoughtfully.

'Supposing, just supposing, I were not engaged to Irene, would you want to get involved with me then? I want the truth, Katarina!'

Kate hesitated.

'If you mean would I go to bed with you, Philip, then the answer's no. I don't ever intend to make love with a man unless I know that he's going to marry me.'

'I see,' said Philip thoughtfully. 'And if you knew that I was a free man and that I wanted to marry you?'

Colour rushed up into Kate's cheeks.

'That's an outrageous question,' she murmured. 'I can't possibly answer it.'

Philip stared at her intently, his gaze resting on her burning cheeks and downcast eyes.

'I think you already have,' he said softly.

Picking up his shirt, he dressed and strode across to the door.

'I'm going into Thessaloníki tomorrow morning to visit Nikos,' he said. 'Would you like to come?'

Kate hesitated.

'Purely a business arrangement,' he assured her. 'You can stock up on film and that sort of thing.'

'All right,' she agreed.

She walked across to the front door of her unit and held it open for him.

'I'll call for you about nine o'clock,' he said and dropped a swift, light kiss on her head.

Neither of them saw the dark-haired girl in the red and white Givenchy dress who had just come round the bend in the path. She stood frozen for a moment and then hurried away, her face distorted with fury.

CHAPTER FOUR

KATE was still drinking coffee when a knock sounded at her front door the following morning. Dabbing at her lips with a napkin, she snatched up her jacket and hurried across the room.

'You're early, Philip!' she said, flinging open the door. 'It's only eight thir—— Oh!'

For it was not Philip who stood there, but Stavros Marmara. Although his eyes were slightly bloodshot, he looked in every other way a picture of healthy young manhood. His olive skin glowed, his limbs were tanned and muscular under white tennis clothes and, as he caught Kate's gaze, his perfect teeth flashed in an engaging smile.

'May I come in?' he asked hesitantly.

'Yes, of course,' said Kate, puzzled. 'Can I get you some coffee?'

'Thanks,' agreed Stavros.

He followed her into the small dining area and hovered nervously while she poured the coffee.

'Do sit down,' she invited. 'Have some rolls, too, if you like.'

'No, thanks. I never really eat breakfast, but the coffee looks fine.'

Kate saw his hesitation and took pity on him.

'Are you calling to ask me to play tennis, or can I do something for you?' she asked.

Stavros let out his breath in a long sigh.

'To be frank, it's a tricky situation,' he admitted, stirring his coffee. 'But I want to begin by apologising to you.'

'Apologising?' echoed Kate in a baffled voice.

75

'Yeah. About the accident yesterday. I guess it was our fault really. We were all totally plastered and we were fooling around in a pretty stupid way, but I never thought anything like that would happen. It's lucky you were there. I'll bet you saved Nikos's life.'

Kate made a small, embarrassed gesture with her hands.

'I only did what anybody else would have done,' she said.

'Anybody who wasn't drunk and totally useless,' corrected Stavros with a shamefaced grimace. 'Anyway, I want you to know Irene and I are very grateful to you. Which makes it even harder to say what I have to say now.'

'Oh?' asked Kate warily.

Stavros's dark eyes met hers for an instant, then flickered uncomfortably away to a point on the wall above her head. He took a quick gulp of his coffee.

'Irene saw Philip leaving your villa last night,' he said bluntly.

It was Kate's turn to look uncomfortable, but somehow she kept at least a partial control on her response. Although her cheeks flamed, her voice was cool and steady as she replied, 'Yes, he came to discuss some business matters with me,' she said. 'He's planning to take me into Thessaloníki to buy some more photographic equipment today.'

'I hope for your sake that's all that he's planning,' rejoined Stavros sombrely.

'I don't know what you mean,' said Kate.

'Look, I don't know how to put this,' continued Stavros, 'but Philip is the kind of guy that likes women. He's had a real harem over the years, but they never meant a damn to him. Sooner or later he's going to marry Irene. Everybody knows that, so normally nobody gets hurt. But you don't seem like the usual kind of woman that he tangles with.'

'Oh. What's that?' demanded Kate.

Stavros shrugged.

'Rich bitches out after a good time,' he said.

'Well, you needn't worry about me,' retorted Kate coolly. 'I'm quite sure that Mr Andronikos has nothing but a professional interest in me, just as I do in him.'

Stavros flung up his hands defensively in front of his face.

'Hey, look, I'm sorry,' he said. 'I guess I was right out of line even to mention it. Anyway, I'm relieved to hear you say that. Irene's been crying her eyes out, worrying about it. You know, she tries to pretend she's so cool and sophisticated, but she's just a baby underneath it all. She's really crazy about Philip and she hates it when he plays around on her.'

He drained the last of his coffee and stood up.

'Well, thanks for putting up with me, Kate,' he said warmly. 'Maybe I'll take you up on that game of tennis one of these days, OK?'

As the door closed behind him, Kate collapsed in a chair, put her hands over her face and shuddered. It was less than a week since she had first met Philip Andronikos, but in that time her world had been turned completely upside-down. She was certain of only one thing—that she felt thoroughly confused and upset. Events were simply moving too fast for her. From the first moment Philip had exerted a powerful magnetic attraction over her, but it was an attraction she distrusted. He projected a strong, almost aggressive aura of virility, but that was not the only basis for Kate's response to him. If the current that passed between them every time they met had been only physical, she would have run a mile.

It was only six months since Leon Clark had let her down so badly, and her feelings were still too raw and confused for her to risk any further disillusionment. Whatever trendy ideas Leon might have had, Kate wanted only the traditional blessings: love and marriage. But was Philip Andronikos really likely to offer them to her? On their first meeting she had glimpsed a quite different side to Philip from the one most people saw. Beneath the tough exterior of the business tycoon there had been a man as sensitive to beauty as she was herself. A man who played the bouzouki with fire and passion, and sang love-songs with a fervour that brought tears to her eyes. And he had other good qualities too. At Porto Carras she had seen his loyalty and affection for the people of Áyios Dimitrios as he'd spoken of his plans for the village.

Yet Philip's loyalty to the traditional Greek customs cut both ways. Kate had no doubt that Philip would make a loyal husband and father when he married. But was he really likely to fly in the face of custom and marry a penniless foreigner? Or was Stavros right? Did Philip see Kate only as another in a long line of women to be used and then discarded? Realism compelled her to admit that it was all too probable. Whatever Philip had hinted at in the heat of passion last night, was he really likely to break his engagement to Irene?

'No,' she said aloud. 'Of course not.'

Despairingly she picked up the coffee percolator and saw her own distorted face staring miserably back at her from its silver surface. Well, it was only too easy to get a distorted view of things when Philip Andronikos was around, but she must keep control of herself. 'I have to remember two things,' she whispered to herself. 'Irene loves him and my relationship with him must be purely a business one.'

When Philip arrived shortly after nine o'clock she was ready and waiting, dressed in her jade-green skirt and blouse, with her camera bag firmly gripped in both hands.

'Hello,' he said, his eyes kindling as they met hers. 'Did you sleep well?'

She gave him a subdued smile and then looked hastily away.

'Yes, thank you,' she said formally. 'Did you?'

He gave her a long, measuring look.

'What's the matter with you?' he demanded.

'Nothing!'

'Then why are you staring at me as if I'm the big, bad wolf?'

'I'm not!' she denied.

His lips set and for a moment he seemed like a stern, unyielding statue carved out of Pentelic marble. Then suddenly his mouth relaxed into a lazy smile.

'Never mind,' he said softly. 'Let's get going.'

For the first hour or so of the drive they chatted easily. In response to Philip's questions Kate told him of her country childhood, of a major bushfire she had filmed for a news bulletin, of the places she had visited in Europe, of various adult-education courses she had studied. In return Philip told her of the triumphs and disasters of his climb from poverty to wealth and she listened, enthralled, feeling as if it were some fairy-tale saga. Somehow she had expected that, after the hard struggle to set up the first Andronikos hotel, everything must have been smooth sailing for him. But Philip's terse account of the setbacks he had suffered made her realise how wrong that was. A major fire, the collapse of a bank, obstruction from local councils and an airline strike had all been just incentives to grit his teeth and keep going. Kate felt a new wave of respect for the man beside her who seemed to radiate vitality, power and determination.

'I don't think anything would stop you from getting what you wanted,' she said as they neared a small picnic spot near Poligiros.

'Probably not,' he agreed wryly. 'Listen, do you mind if we stop for a few minutes? I need a break.'

'Of course not,' agreed Kate.

Philip pulled the car to a halt next to a picnic table and climbed out. Then he stretched slowly, flinging up one arm to massage the tension out of his neck muscles. Kate watched those deft, powerful fingers at work and felt a tremor of longing shoot through her. Philip caught her gaze and smiled wickedly.

'If you had any heart you'd do this for me,' he grumbled. 'What I really need is a woman's touch.'

'What you really need is a strait-jacket,' retorted Kate, backing away.

One tanned, muscular arm shot out and caught her firmly by the shoulder.

'I thought you said you once did a course in Swedish massage,' he said. 'All I'm asking for is a neck rub. I was working on that damned computer until three a.m. last night and I've got a pain like a knife in the back of my neck.'

'Truly?' asked Kate suspiciously.

'Truly,' agreed Philip.

'All right, but don't try anything on,' she warned. 'You'd better take your jacket off.'

Philip sat on the bench with his elbows in the picnic table.

'Now close your eyes,' she instructed.

'Close my...? Well, you're the boss.'

'It's all part of the treatment,' Kate assured him. 'Take a deep breath and let it out slowly. Now what can you hear?'

'Nothing.'

'Listen harder,' she instructed.

Philip was silent for a moment. Kate stood in front of him and watched until he relaxed, but an alert expression slowly replaced the tension in his face.

'Wind in the trees,' he murmured. 'Birdsong, a goat's bell in the distance.'

'Good,' she said in a satisfied voice, moving round behind him. 'What can you smell?'

Resting her forearms on his shoulders, she leant forwards so that her weight gently eased his shoulders down, breaking the tension in them.

'Mmm. Pine needles,' he said. 'Some kind of aromatic vegetation. Hot, dry earth.'

With relaxed open hands Kate stroked firmly up Philip's back on either side of his spine. When she reached the shoulders she pulled them down gently, then stroked outwards, curving her hands round the tops of his arms and gliding lightly down the sides. She repeated this several times, then kneaded his shoulders thoroughly and applied pressure with her thumbs on either side of his spine. Only when she heard him sigh and felt his muscles relax under her fingers did she turn her attention to his neck. Supporting his forehead with one hand, she massaged the back of his neck slowly with the other. Then she used the flat of her hands to make circular pressures all over his hair, followed by a brisk scalp rub with her fingertips. Lastly, with open hands she did a fast, springy hacking movement across the shoulders and finished up by stroking his neck and back as if she were smoothing a cat's fur.

'There. How does that feel?' she asked.

He opened his eyes and looked around him.

'Incredible,' he admitted. 'I can't believe how it makes me feel. I started to notice all sorts of things that I wasn't aware of before. Like the roughness of the table under my elbows, the sound of a bee buzzing in the bushes. Things I was screening out because I was too busy thinking about work. You're amazing, Katarina, you really are.'

Kate shrugged self-consciously.

'Well, to finish it off you really ought to look around you and see what you notice now that your eyes are open again,' she suggested.

With a thoughtful expression Philip looked around him.

'Blue sky,' he said. 'Olive groves in the distance. Lots of shrubs. Holly oaks, see, with their little acorns on them? Pink oleanders that have almost finished flowering. And arbutus bushes. We used to eat the berries off those when I was a child in Áyios Dimitrios. They're a bit like strawberries, but with a rougher texture. Here, try one.'

He reached out and plucked one of the rough orange-coloured fruits from a bush and slipped it between Kate's parted lips. She swallowed and felt the sweet, knobbly berry slip down her throat. But Philip was already crouched at the base of the arbutus bushes, peering at something on the ground.

'Look, crocuses,' he exclaimed. 'Yellow crocuses, and I didn't even notice them.'

He rose to his feet and took a step closer to Kate. His brown fingers smoothed back her auburn curls. For an instant he stood there, looking at her with an intent, urgent gaze as if he was taking in every detail of her small, straight nose, her smooth creamy skin, her troubled green eyes.

'You make me feel as if I'd been born blind,' he said softly.

Then he kissed her with an intensity that made her pulses leap and her whole body ache to be united with his. It took a powerful effort of will to clench her fists and thrust him away.

'Don't, Philip!' she cried. 'I don't want to be one of your harem.'

'One of my what?' demanded Philip with an incredulous expression.

'Your harem...the women you just use and abandon.'

The tension was back in Philip's face.

'Who told you this?' he demanded.

Kate was frightened by the anger that blazed suddenly in his liquid dark eyes.

'What does it matter?' she asked defensively.

'Who told you?' he insisted, clutching her arm.

'S-Stavros.'

Philip swore violently in Greek. Kate did not recognise the word, but there was no mistaking the intonation.

'When did Stavros have the chance to have such a conversation with you?' he demanded.

'He came to my villa this morning,' faltered Kate.

'I see,' said Philip grimly. 'And told you I had a harem?'

'He said you'd been having affairs for years, but it didn't mean anything, because everybody knew you'd marry Irene in the end and usually nobody got hurt. But he said I was different from most of your women.'

Philip groaned.

'Is it true, then?' demanded Kate.

'Yes and no,' said Philip through gritted teeth. 'For heaven's sake, Katarina, try and understand! This match with Irene was arranged fourteen years ago. Was I supposed to live like a monk all that time?'

Kate swallowed hard, trying to fight back the sense of desolation that overwhelmed her.

'So Stavros was right?' she asked huskily. 'You were just going to use me and then abandon me?'

'No!' cried Philip. 'Look, Katarina, Stavros is a master of lies and distortions. And he's even better when it comes to twisting the truth to serve his own ends. He's just trying to poison your mind against me.'

'How do I know that you're not just trying to poison my mind against him?' retaliated Kate. 'You admit that everything he's said is true, so why shouldn't I believe him?'

'Because he's no good!' shouted Philip. 'He trades on that clean-cut, handsome, smiling image, but underneath you can't trust him. I don't want you to have any more to do with him, Katarina. Is that clear?'

Kate choked with disbelief and indignation.

'No, it isn't!' she fumed. 'Since when do you have the right to pick and choose who I can associate with? And what's Stavros done that's so terrible anyway?'

'I'm not prepared to reveal that,' said Philip bleakly. 'There are things I know about him that even his mother doesn't know, and heaven forbid that she ever should. In some ways I feel responsible. I persuaded her to send him to the States for his education, but he got in with a very wild crowd there. Kids with far too much money and not enough guidance. You will just have to believe me when I say that you must not have anything to do with him.'

Kate was shaken, but she tried not to show it. After all, Philip had offered her no proof that what he said was true. She thought again of Stavros's hesitant, boyish smile and shook her head in a dazed way.

'I can't believe what you're telling me, Philip,' she said. 'But, even if it's true, it doesn't change anything. I mean, basically Stavros is right. I'm not just a good-time girl. I hate to think of Irene crying her eyes out last night because she knew you'd been with me.'

Philip looked incredulous.

'Irene doing what?' he demanded.

'Crying her eyes out,' faltered Kate. 'Well, that's what Stavros said!'

Philip chuckled grimly.

'If it's any consolation to you,' he said, 'I can tell you now that Irene was in the main bar of the reception centre until well after midnight last night. She seemed to be in perfectly good spirits to me, drinking Brandy Alexanders and flirting with Yves Sauvignon. If you'd just open your eyes, Katarina, you'd see quite clearly that Irene is no more in love with me than I am with her!'

Kate shrugged wearily.

'Maybe you're right, Philip,' she admitted. 'But you are engaged to her. And as long as that's true I don't think it's right for me to have any relationship with you except a business one. It's as simple as that.'

'Life is never that simple!' retorted Philip savagely. 'I wish it were. But, if it's complicated or not, I fell in love with you from the moment I first saw you, Katarina. And, one way or another, I intend to have you.'

His eyes narrowed as he said this, and Kate realised that his fingers were digging into her arms. A wave of emotion washed over her so that she could scarcely breathe.

'You're hurting me,' she whispered.

He released her instantly.

'I'll never do that,' he promised passionately. 'But just tell me this, Katarina: if it hadn't been for Irene would you let yourself go? Would you fall in love with me?'

His eyes were intent and searching, demanding the truth from her. For an instant she evaded him, her heart racing. She heard the shrilling of insects, leaves rustling in the breeze, saw the crocuses like yellow stars beneath the bushes. Then his hard fingers caught her chin and turned her face up to his. She gazed at him earnestly.

'You know I would, Philip,' she murmured.

He caught her against him for a moment and she felt the smooth fabric of his linen jacket against her cheek.

'That's all I needed to know,' he said exultantly. 'Come, Katarina. Let's go to Thessaloníki.'

After the sunlit silences of the Halkidiki peninsula, the roar of Thessaloníki was almost deafening. Kate was conscious only of a concrete jungle of apartment buildings, bristling television aerials, blaring horns and petrol fumes, but somehow in Philip's company all this uproar and overcrowding seemed invigorating and full of vitality. At the hospital they were turned away and asked to come back later to see Nikos, so they spent time shopping and strolling. Philip took her to see the Arch of Galerius, which was so blackened by petrol fumes that many of the carvings were scarcely visible. Then he left her in the Ethnological and Popular Art Museum for an hour while he saw his lawyer on business. After that they ate a light snack in the OTE tower, which was a soaring futuristic building with a panoramic view over the city. When their feet were thoroughly rested they plunged back into the bustle of the city.

'Well,' said Philip, 'what would you like to do now?'

'I'd better buy some film,' replied Kate. 'Can you find me a cheap photographic supply store?'

'I think so,' said Philip. 'On one condition.'

'What's that?' she asked curiously.

'That you also let me buy you some new clothes.'

'Oh, Philip, I couldn't,' objected Kate. 'It wouldn't seem right.'

'Why not?' demanded Philip. 'After all, you ruined your clothes yesterday helping Nikos, and I feel responsible for that. Besides, you'll need an evening dress for the opening of the hotel in a couple of weeks' time. I can't have my official photographer turning up in jeans and a T-shirt amid all the beautiful people, can I?'

Kate looked at him suspiciously.

'I think I'm being conned,' she said.

'Go on. Give in and enjoy it!' urged Philip. 'I'd love to buy some really elegant clothes for you.'

'Well, only if you take it out of my salary,' she conceded at last.

Two hours and many parcels later they sat down at a street-side table in Platia Aristotelous on the waterfront for a late lunch. The air was mild and humid, and the sea glowed bronze and pink and lavender under a pastel sky.

'Well, did you enjoy yourself?' asked Philip.

Kate groaned.

'It was wonderful,' she admitted. 'And I'm so thrilled with that gold dress, but I'll have to work for the next hundred years to pay you back.'

Philip's eyes kindled as they rested on her eager face.

'I rather like the idea of having you around for the next hundred years,' he said. 'Especially if you have to do my bidding every minute of the time. Now just let me take a quick look at the financial papers and then we'll order some lunch.'

Kate was sipping a gin and tonic and watching the passers-by when she heard his sudden intake of breath a moment later.

'What is it?' she asked.

Philip was frowning down at one of the folded newspapers, but he looked up as she spoke.

'Hmm? Oh, sorry. Just a paragraph in here about a business associate of mine, Hristos Hionides. He's the major backer of the Hotel Ariadne. Apparently he's suffered a heart attack.'

'Oh, I'm sorry,' said Kate, seeing Philip's preoccupied frown. 'You seem very shocked. Was he a close friend of yours?'

'No,' replied Philip slowly. 'But it does give me a bit of a jolt. Hristos isn't very old, only forty-five or so, and he seemed perfectly healthy last time I saw him. And of course this sort of thing won't do his business much good. It always makes investors panic and share prices go down when somebody important gets sick.'

'Will it affect your business?' asked Kate. 'I mean the hotel loan or anything like that?'

'Good heavens, no,' said Philip. 'At least, not unless Hristos dies and his executors foreclose on the mortgage. But that's not terribly likely. No, it's just another reminder of my own mortality, I suppose. Never mind. What would you like for lunch?'

They ate charcoal-grilled octopus on a bed of lettuce with quarters of tangy lemon and an assortment of salads and dips, followed by coffee and chocolate halva. As Kate bit into a cube of the gritty, sweet sesame paste, a smile softened the corners of her mouth. It's all so complicated, she thought ruefully. Philip is going to marry

Irene, I'm not really sure that he loves me, and yet somehow I feel happier than I've ever felt in my life before. She looked up and caught his gaze on hers, tender, amused, encouraging. He reached for his glass and his hand touched hers briefly, as if he had read her mind.

'Don't worry, we'll work it out somehow,' he said softly. 'Now, if you've finished, we'll go and see Nikos. And after that I'll pay a quick visit to my lawyer and then we'll go home.'

At the hospital they found Nikos drowsy but comfortable with one arm swathed in bandages, and Anna sitting in a chair next to his bed, gyrating in time to a Walkman attached to her head. When she caught sight of Philip and Kate she paid them the supreme compliment of pulling off the transistor radio and coming to greet them. Her face lit up and she flung her arms around Kate.

'*Efharisto, efharisto!*' she said fervently. 'Nikos tell me what you do, miss. You save his life. We all thank you very, very much. My mother, my father, me. You come visit us at Áyios Dimitrios; we cook you meal, yes?'

'Thank you, Anna,' said Kate, smiling. 'I'd be honoured.'

Nikos too had to haul himself up on to his pillows and offer his thanks in a slurred voice, but, seeing how the effort exhausted him, Kate soon caught Philip's eyes and made an excuse to leave.

It was late afternoon when they finally reached home. On the way Philip suggested a visit to the Petralona Caves and they spent a fascinating hour wandering through the echoing caverns, where prehistoric men had sheltered during a vanished Ice Age. Afterwards, when they emerged on the terrace outside, Philip laid one hand casually on Kate's shoulder.

'Well, did you enjoy that?' he asked.

'Oh, yes!' agreed Kate enthusiastically. 'I'd love to come back some time and take photos of it. It's an intriguing place, isn't it? The floodlighting was wonderful. It made the stalactites look so mysterious and strange. And I loved the exhibits too—the bone tools and the woolly rhinoceros remains and those pathetic little replicas of the cavemen curled up in a corner, trying to shelter their children. I suppose you've seen it lots of times, but it was really something special for me.'

'Actually I've never been there in my life before,' confessed Philip.

'Really?' exclaimed Kate. 'Why ever not?'

He ruffled her hair pensively and smiled.

'I suppose I was always too busy working,' he said half to himself. 'And there was nobody that I wanted to do things with before. Nobody special.'

Kate gave him a small, troubled smile. His words touched her to the quick, but she was too level-headed to forget the existence of Irene. The outlook from the terrace in front of the caves was breathtaking—a luminous panorama of dark hills, slender cypresses and the distant sea. Philip's hand still rested casually on her shoulder, and she longed to move into the warmth of his embrace and stand beside him enjoying the view, but, with an effort of will, she broke free.

'We'd better go home,' she said in a stifled voice. 'It'll be dark soon.'

He gave her an odd look, but followed her down the path to the car without making any reply. Yet he was clearly in no hurry to get home, for when they reached the last bend in the road above Áyios Dimitrios just before sunset he pulled the car on to the grassy verge and climbed out.

'There's something I want to show you,' he said gruffly. 'Will you come and look?'

Warily Kate climbed out of the car and joined him on the hillside. The air was fragrant with the scent of wild marjoram, and the scene stretched out below them was amazingly beautiful, with the white buildings of the hotel gleaming against the dark blue backdrop of the sea. Philip stood for a long time, drinking in the view, and she saw the furrows in his brow slowly relax as he took in his breath and let it out in a long sigh. At last, without turning his head, he reached out one strong brown hand and groped for her fingers. He held her hand in a grip so tight that it was almost painful and, sensing the tension in him, Kate instinctively moved closer and laid her cheek on his arm.

'What is it?' she murmured.

'Oh, Katarina, Katarina,' he said hoarsely, 'how can I tell you what I'm feeling? When I was a poor boy, herding goats with no shoes and not enough to eat, I used to climb up to this spot and look down on the village, and I used to make myself a promise. I used to close my eyes and wish as hard as if I were fighting for my life that my dreams would come true. And this was my wish and the promise that I made myself: that one day I would pull Áyios Dimitrios out of its poverty with my bare hands; I would build a fine hotel down there, right where you see it now, and nobody from my village would ever go hungry again; they would all have jobs and shoes and proper houses, and a doctor when they were sick and a school for the children. That was my dream.'

His voice was so full of pain that Kate stared at him in bewilderment.

'But you've done it,' she reminded him. 'You should be so proud of yourself, Philip. You did everything you promised yourself that you would do. In a couple of weeks the hotel will be opening and your dream will all be true.'

Philip heaved a sigh and his grip tightened, crushing her fingers in his.

'Yes, but perhaps dreams are only worth having if there is somebody to share them,' he said heavily. 'You know, Katarina, for a long time now I've been very pleased with myself. Each year my bank balance grew bigger, I owned more property, I worked longer and longer hours and I had the pick of the most desirable women in Europe. Of course, I promised myself that one fine day I would slow down, marry and enjoy what I had amassed. But I didn't realise how frantic and empty my life had become until an earthquake hit me.'

'An earthquake?' faltered Kate.

Philip's features creased into a tense smile.

'Yes,' he said. 'Only a few days ago, and the aftershocks are still disturbing me. Oh, it wasn't the trembling of the ground that upset me. That was a very minor matter. It was the upheaval in my own heart when I met a certain wild-eyed, tear-stained Australian girl on a mountainside. A girl who seemed to turn all my previous ideas and my good opinion of myself upside-down.'

'W-what do you mean?' whispered Kate.

Philip's painful grip on her fingers slowly relaxed, and he reached up and tidied her straying auburn curls.

'Simply that I've been dreaming about the wrong things,' he said softly. 'Oh, the Hotel Ariadne would be a fine dream if I had somebody to share it with. But not nearly such a fine dream as the two you showed me yesterday.'

'I don't understand,' breathed Kate.

Philip's lips twisted.

'I'm talking about the photos you showed me,' he explained. 'The photos of those two old people who could face a hard road serenely just because they were together, and that young mother who knew that love was more important than money. I've been dreaming the wrong dreams for years now, Kate. No wonder you think that I'm selfish and arrogant.'

'I don't!' protested Kate fervently.

'Then what are your real feelings towards me?' demanded Philip.

Kate swallowed painfully as a rush of emotion swept over her. She thought of Philip comforting her after the earthquake, his anguish when he thought she had been shot, the passionate fervour of his kisses, the heady excitement of being in his company. Then she did something which surprised them both. Catching his face in her hands, she drew his head down to hers and kissed him fiercely on the mouth.

'I love you,' she said in a low, throbbing voice. 'But we both know it's hopeless!'

Then she fled back to the car. But as she reached it, Philip came after her and caught her by the wrist. He was breathing heavily as if he had been running.

'Nothing is hopeless!' he contradicted her fiercely. 'If you want it badly enough you can have anything in the world. Anything, Katarina!'

CHAPTER FIVE

THE next two weeks were a difficult time for Kate. As far as her work was concerned she had seldom been so contented in her life before. Philip had been delighted with the photos of the yacht, exclaiming that they were far too good for mere insurance records, and Kate was now happily engaged in working on the tourist brochures. Each day she went out at sunrise and spent hours fiddling with her tripod and filters and light meter to try and capture the unique beauty of Áyios Dimitrios. She had fallen in love with the place, and her photos reflected the fact. Print after print revealed the lyrical magic of its rose-tinted sunrises, the rugged grandeur of its steep blue hillsides, the tough, humorous vitality of its people. But, if Kate's work was giving her more satisfaction than ever before, her emotions were another matter entirely.

After the trip to Thessaloníki she had made a determined resolution to stay away from Philip Andronikos. Yet she was miserably aware that a moth might just as well have made a resolution to stay away from a candle. She had already fluttered too close to that glowing flame and been painfully burnt. She knew she could not risk any further encounters. Consequently whenever Philip made his way up the pine-carpeted pathway to her villa she was always either 'just going out to take some photos' or 'too busy developing films to stop and chat'. But her pretence fooled neither of them. Whenever she found herself in a large group with Philip she could not prevent her gaze from straying longingly over his face, and once or twice she looked up to find his smouldering brown eyes trained thoughtfully on her. It was probably a good thing that these chance meetings were rare. Philip was now so busy preparing for the hotel opening that he seldom surfaced except for snatched meals in the staff dining-room. And Kate herself was working nearly as hard. Keeping busy helped to still the intolerable ache that spread through her body whenever she realised that her time at Áyios Dimitrios would soon be over and she would have to leave.

On the morning of the official opening Kate was woken by a timid knock at her bedroom door.

'Yasu,' said a vaguely familiar voice.

'Yasu,' she replied sleepily, sitting up and pushing her hair out of her eyes. 'Oh, Anna, it's you! Whatever have you got there?'

Anna set the laden tray down on Kate's bedside table and beamed.

'Loukoumathes,' she said proudly. 'Not from chef either. Anna make them.'

'Loukou...?' queried Kate.

'Loukoumathes,' repeated Anna slowly and carefully. 'You look.'

Kate stared down at the tray. A thick white plate, which obviously had a much humbler origin than the kitchens of the Hotel Ariadne, was loaded with crispy golden dumplings soaked in honey.

'You like?' asked Anna eagerly. 'I make for you because you save my brother.'

'Oh, Anna, how kind!' exclaimed Kate. 'They look delicious!'

Anna watched approvingly as Kate ate the plateful of dumplings and drank two cups of coffee. Then she produced a flat parcel wrapped in tissue paper.

'This for you too,' she said, smiling.

Kate unwrapped the parcel and gasped.

'But Anna! These are handmade lace curtains. They must have taken you months and months of work!'

Anna nodded proudly.

'I make for my dowry,' she acknowledged. 'But now they are for you. For your dowry.'

Kate was tempted to refuse, to say that she could not possibly accept such a beautiful and valuable gift. But then she realised what an insult that would be. It was precisely because they were so beautiful and valuable that Anna was offering them to her.

'Thank you, Anna,' she said sincerely. 'They are wonderful. I will cherish them.'

The two girls gazed at each other with respect, then Anna smiled.

'I work now,' she said.

Kate sat gazing at the curtains for a couple of minutes, then set them down thoughtfully on her pillow and climbed out of bed. She could hear Anna humming as she scrubbed out the bath. Thoughtfully she rummaged through her bag and then went through to the bathroom.

'Anna,' she said hesitantly, 'I'd like to give you something too. Will you accept this tape?'

Anna looked down delightedly at the cassette which Kate was holding out to her. It was a collection of Bruce Springsteen hits.

'OK,' she agreed jauntily. 'Very nice.'

She mimed putting on a Walkman and doing some energetic dancing and they both laughed. Anna gestured at the evening dress which was hanging up in the bathroom.

'*Oraia,*' she said admiringly. 'Very fine. You wear this with it tonight?'

She picked up the expensive perfume atomiser which was part of the complimentary equipment of every suite at the Hotel Ariadne. Kate shook her head ruefully.

'I can't,' she said. 'I'm allergic to it. *Alleryika?*'

Anna nodded with sudden comprehension.

'Ah,' she said.

'Look,' said Kate, struck by a sudden thought. 'Why don't you take it, Anna? And the talcum powder too. I can't use it!'

She bundled the toiletries up and thrust them into Anna's hands.

'*Endaxi?*' she asked. 'OK?'

Anna smiled like a conspirator.

'*Endaxi,*' she agreed. 'I wear to party. Very big party at Áyios Dimitrios today. You go to the opening ball tonight, miss?'

'I wouldn't miss it for the world!' said Kate.

There was a very big party everywhere on the hotel estate that day. The village was celebrating in its own style with spit-roasted lamb, loud bouzouki music and traditional dancing, while the hotel itself was bursting with activity. Special charter flights had flown into Thessaloníki in the morning, and coach-loads of guests kept arriving all day. For the first time the restaurants and lobbies and swimming-pools were thronged with people, laughing and enjoying themselves. A Greek band played on the terrace by the waterfront, and a mini-regatta was going on in the bay with the *Eleftheria* acting as flagship. But the real highlight was to be the official opening dinner and ball in the main reception centre.

As she slipped into her gold evening dress shortly after seven o'clock Kate found that her hands were shaking slightly with nerves. For the first time she wondered anxiously just what part she was to play in the festivities. Philip had made some joking remark about not wanting his official photographer dressed in jeans and a T-shirt, but he had never told her what photographs he wanted her to take. What was even worse, she had no idea of whether she was supposed to be taking part in the official dinner for invited dignitaries or whether she would be part of the celebration in the staff dining-room instead. She could not help remembering the unpleasant scene on the yacht when Irene had ordered her to go back with the crew where she belonged. If only she knew where she did belong! One thing was certain at any rate: it would be Irene Marmara who stood smiling radiantly at Philip's side all evening and not Kate Walsh.

As Kate made her way down the winding path to the reception centre she heard the muted hum of a large party gradually warming up. A sudden thump followed by a whizzing shriek made her jump back in alarm, until she realised that it was only the start of the fireworks display. A rocket exploded overhead in a shower of pink and green sparks, lighting up the dark blue sea and sending magical flickers of colour over the white buildings ahead. Somewhere in front of her she could hear the wild rhythmic clapping that generally accompanied a Greek dancing display, and for no accountable reason her spirits suddenly lifted. Never mind about Irene or Philip. The smartest thing she could do tonight was simply to relax and enjoy herself. Hitching her camera strap more firmly on to her shoulder, she marched boldly forward to the side-door of the reception centre.

'*Yasu*, Kate.'

'*Ya*,' said Kate, grateful to see a familiar face.

It was Dorothea Zografou, the deputy manager of the hotel, dressed in a long, shimmering pink gown with a spray of orchids on her left shoulder and her greying brown hair swept into a smart chignon. However, Kate noticed that Dorothea still wore her small hotel identity-badge, clipped to her right shoulder.

'Dorothea,' she entreated, 'can you tell me where I should be? Philip did say something about my being an official photographer tonight, but he hasn't told me what photos to take or where to go. I don't even know if I'm meant to be attending the guests' dinner or not.'

Dorothea frowned thoughtfully.

'You were certainly on the guest list,' she said, 'although not at the official table, of course. Just a moment, Kate.'

She moved across to a side-table laden with flowers and picked up a seating plan.

'You're at the Press table,' she said, 'with the rest of the journalists and photographers. Philip already has two photographers hired to do publicity photos, so I think it's up to you what shots you take. But just one word of warning, Kate: if any of the journalists try to pump you for copy about his private life, don't say a word. Nothing infuriates him worse than having his personal life splashed all over the tabloids.'

'Thanks, Dorothea,' agreed Kate. 'I'll remember.'

Dorothea smiled. 'Well, I'd better go and take my place in the reception line,' she said hastily. 'I think the mayor of Sarti is just arriving. Have a good time, Kate.'

Kate watched the older woman thread her way through the milling crowds in the main lobby, and suddenly her heart leapt. Philip was standing in the midst of a throng of men in evening suits and women dressed in glittering finery. Kate recognised a star from a major US television series, a Greek politician who had been at the heart of a bribery scandal and a well-known shipping magnate. Then suddenly all the other faces slipped out of focus, for Philip's eyes met hers. It was as if they were alone in the room or alone on a wild mountainside. Her gaze locked with his and she felt a powerful current of feeling surge between them. I love you, Philip, she thought urgently and knew that he had heard that silent cry. Then casually, almost contemptuously, he looked away from her, only to smile down enchantingly at Irene, who was clinging to his arm. Kate felt so wounded that she could scarcely breathe as flashbulbs lit up all around, capturing the happy couple on film. Was this how Philip wanted her to spend the rest of her life? she wondered indignantly. As the silent, watchful mistress, pushed into the wings while the true wife basked in the limelight? Well, damn him!

As the evening wore on Kate's uneasiness increased. The chefs at the Hotel Ariadne were determined to display their prowess, and course after course of delicious food was whisked in from the kitchens. Charcoal-grilled pitta bread accompanied dips of shrimp, smoked cod's roe, chick-peas and creamed aubergines. There were entrées of grilled octopus and calamari garnished with lettuce and quartered tomatoes, Cretan sausages, little triangles of pastry filled with cheese or spinach, and vast silver chafing dishes containing a dazzling array of main courses—spit-roasted lamb, aromatic beef stew in a tomato base, charcoal-grilled chicken and seafood platters. And these were followed by elaborate desserts of honey-soaked pastry crammed with nuts, ices made from mouthwatering fruits and intricately decorated cakes. But Kate scarcely noticed the food. She was too busy watching Philip and Irene.

To her disquiet, they seemed to be on the best of terms. Whenever a camera flashed Philip seemed to be laying a hand caressingly on Irene's arm or bending his head attentively to listen to her chatter. And, when the official opening finally took place and a crowd of well-wishers surged forward at the end of the dinner, Philip put his arm around Irene's shoulders and led her into the centre of the dance-floor. Then he motioned to a waiter with a tray and champagne to join them.

'Ladies and gentlemen,' he said in his deep, resonant voice, 'you all know that the opening of the Hotel Ariadne at Áyios Dimitrios represents a dream come true to me. I don't want to slow up the party, but before we get back to enjoying ourselves I would like to take a moment to remember two fine men from this village who made the fulfilment of this dream a possibility. Sadly, Con Marmara and Aristo Andronikos are no longer with us in the flesh, but I am sure they are here tonight in spirit. Ladies and gentlemen, will you drink a toast with me? To Con and Aristo!'

'To Con and Aristo!' murmured everybody obediently, lifting their glasses.

But that wasn't the end of it. For Philip beckoned another waiter who was hovering in the background.

'And, since Con is not able to be here himself, I would like to present his daughter Irene with a small gift in recognition of all that I owe to the Marmara family.'

The waiter came forward with a red velvet jewellery box, which he opened to display a shimmering diamond necklace. There was a concerted gasp of admiration as Philip drew the gleaming cascade of gems from their resting place and fastened them around Irene's throat. Then he kissed her softly on the cheek.

'Meya!' he said. 'Wear it in good health!'

Kate felt as if she had been pushed off a cliff as the crowd of journalists at her table surged forward to snap photos of the big event. No doubt Philip was only right to honour Con Marmara, but he could hardly have made a more public show of his commitment to Irene if he had married her tonight. Kate recalled Stavros's warnings about Philip's character, and a wave of bitterness flooded through her. You fool! she thought. You really believed he loved you, didn't you?

'Hey, are you all right?' asked a voice behind her. 'You look kinda pale.'

'Oh, Stavros. No, I'm fine,' lied Kate desperately. 'I just have a slight headache. I think I'll go back to my villa now.'

Stavros's hand closed warningly on her arm.

'Don't do that,' he urged in a low voice. 'You'll attract too much attention. Hold your head up and stick it out.'

Somehow, although her heart felt ready to burst, Kate found herself led out on to the dance-floor and whirled professionally around in Stavros's practised embrace. She saw Irene and Philip spin past them, and Philip's gaze met hers with a flare of jealousy that turned to smiling blandness as Irene looked up at him and made some remark. As the music came to an end Stavros led her off the floor and excused himself for a moment. Kate threaded her way through a jungle-like arrangement of potted palms towards her seat, and found herself face to face with Philip.

'I thought I told you to stay away from Stavros!' he hissed with a swift glance at the Press table a few yards away.

'What's it to do with you?' she retorted under her breath.

One of the photographers at the table gave them an interested glance and rose to his feet.

'Pardon me,' he said with the air of a bloodhound sniffing a trail, 'but didn't I see you two lunching together in Platia Aristotelous two weeks ago?'

Kate said nothing but cast Philip a challenging look. His rage melted instantly away, to be replaced by a smiling indifference.

'You may well have done,' he agreed in a bored voice. 'I frequently lunch with my employees when I want to discuss business. Miss Walsh has been doing some publicity photos for the Hotel Ariadne for me, but, of course, she'll be leaving any day now. Oh, do excuse me, won't you? I see Irene is looking rather lost without me.'

'Oh, so there's nothing between you two?' demanded the photographer in disappointed tones.

'No. Absolutely nothing!' agreed Kate bitterly.

And she stormed away to rejoin Stavros.

'I did try to warn you,' said Stavros in a subdued voice with a glance back at the photographer. 'Philip was only playing games with you, honey, but you don't want those goddamned reporters putting two and two together to make five. Act as if you're interested in me and maybe it'll throw them off the scent. OK?'

Kate's eyes filled with angry tears, but she couldn't help seeing the sense in what Stavros said.

'OK,' she agreed sulkily.

As time wore on, her ruffled feelings were soothed a little by Stavros's attentions. She could not help but feel a blazing rage at Philip's callous betrayal, and there was a certain satisfaction in flaunting her pleasure in Stavros's company at the man who had wounded her so deeply. Several times as she sailed around the dance-floor in Stavros's arms she felt Philip's gaze scorching her like a beam from a laser. And, when Stavros made a whispered suggestion that they should go out on the terrace and look at the moonlight over the gulf, she was only too happy to agree.

The moonlight was certainly beautiful. The sea lay spread out below them like a sheet of beaten silver, and the stars blazed in the dark sky overhead. Kate could not help but recall a very similar evening she had spent with Philip three weeks before in Áyia Sofía. Her cheeks flushed hotly at the memory. And when Stavros made no attempt to take her in his arms and kiss her she was not sure whether to feel glad or sorry. It would certainly be a fitting revenge on Philip, but the dreadful truth was that she only wanted to feel one man's arms around her. And Stavros was not the man. She clenched her hands so hard on the stone balustrade that her fingers hurt.

'Don't take it so hard,' urged Stavros. 'He'll be round looking for you again tomorrow. And, anyway, you could hardly expect him to acknowledge his mistress in public when the Press were there, could you?'

'I'm not his mistress!' flared Kate.

'Aren't you?' said Stavros curiously. 'Hell, I'm sorry; I thought by now... Oh, well. That's OK, then, isn't it? If you're not his mistress then you're not going to get hurt, are you?'

'No,' said Kate in a choking voice.

But she knew she was lying. She was already so badly hurt that she couldn't bear another moment of it.

'I'm leaving as soon as I finish the photos,' she continued bleakly.

Stavros squeezed her hand briefly.

'That's probably the best thing,' he agreed soberly. 'For you, for Irene, for everyone. But try not to take it so much to heart, Kate. It would only have been a light-hearted affair for Philip, and it's not worth breaking your heart over.'

Kate swallowed hard.

'I suppose you're right,' she sighed. 'But why are you being so nice to me about it, Stavros? You're Irene's brother. You must absolutely hate me!'

Stavros shrugged.

'Hell, no!' he said with embarrassment. 'I think you're a real nice girl, Kate. I'd like to be friends with you. Look, I'll tell you what. Why don't you and I go for a walk tomorrow up into the hills? Nothing special, just an old-fashioned hike and a picnic?'

Kate thought for a moment, but, after all, what was the alternative? Staying in her villa and crying her eyes out?

'All right,' she agreed tonelessly.

It was nearly six o'clock the following evening when Kate got back to her villa, and she knew at once that something was wrong. The front door was wide open and a tense, angry figure sat at her dining table, like a jungle cat ready to pounce.

'Philip!' she exclaimed in bewilderment. 'What are you doing here?'

'You'll know soon enough!' replied Philip, unsmiling. 'Be good enough to come inside and shut the door. I have things I wish to say to you in private.'

She looked uncertainly at Stavros, who was lounging beside her in the doorway with a ghost of a smile playing around the corners of his mouth.

'I'll stay if you want me to, Kate,' he offered.

'You'll get out of here and fast!' said Philip, springing to his feet in a single movement which took him across the floor. 'I'll speak to you later, Stavros, and I can promise you now it won't be an experience you'll enjoy. Now take yourself off before I throw you out!'

With a faint, mocking lift of his eyebrows and a wink at Kate, Stavros turned and walked away. Left alone with Philip, Kate found that her pulse was beating frantically with apprehension. The man who faced her seemed like a total stranger, with his bronzed, hairy arms folded uncompromisingly across his body, his eyes narrowed into glittering dark slits and his mouth set in a stern line.

'Sit down!' he growled.

'Why should I?' flared Kate. 'I don't take orders from you or anybody else!'

'Oh, don't you?' snarled Philip.

Picking her up bodily, he thrust her into one of the dining chairs and held her there. Her heart beat more tumultuously than ever. His grip was so tight that it was painful, and yet she could not suppress a pang of excitement at his nearness. The raw, arrogant power of his masculinity had never been more apparent. It both thrilled and frightened her.

'You're hurting me!' she whispered breathlessly.

He released her at once.

'I'm sorry,' he said abruptly, rising to his feet. 'I didn't intend to do that. But we need to talk.'

He took in a long, agonised gulp of air, like a man who had just come up from a dive that tested all his strength.

'What about?' demanded Kate warily.

Philip stabbed at the air with his forefinger in the direction of the door where Stavros had just made his exit.

'About that good-for-nothing young scoundrel who's been worming his way into your life!' he retorted.

He paced angrily back across the room and slammed his hand down on the dining table.

'Did he kiss you?' he demanded abruptly. 'Did he caress you?'

'No!' snapped Kate. 'Although I don't see that it's any of your business anyway.'

Philip gave a slight smile and relaxed fractionally.

'No, I suppose he wouldn't,' he murmured half to himself. 'He has subtler ways of ruining people. Where did he take you today?'

Kate shrugged. 'For a picnic in the hills,' she replied warily. 'And then for coffee in the village. Why?'

'Coffee!' Philip pounced on the statement. 'Where did you have coffee?'

'In the coffee-house, of course,' said Kate in bewilderment.

Philip groaned.

'Look, would you mind telling me what this inquisition is about?' she demanded with a touch of heat. 'Anyone would think I'd gone into the men's bath-house the way you're carrying on.'

'You might as well have done!' retorted Philip fiercely. 'Don't you understand anything about Greek village life, Katarina? The *cafeneion* is for men, not women! Stavros understands that, even if you don't. Only a woman who was signalling her availability to every man would go into such a place.'

Kate flinched, but stood her ground.

'Well, how was I to know?' she demanded belligerently. 'Anyway, I doubt if Stavros even thought about it. He's been living in the States for years. He's probably forgotten how primitive people's ideas are here.'

'He has forgotten nothing!' roared Philip. 'He did it only to ruin your reputation among the villagers, and it's just not good enough, Katarina. I warned you about Stavros and I won't have you associating with him!'

'Oh, won't you?' cried Kate, starting to her feet. 'Won't you just? Well, it may have escaped your notice, but I'm twenty-six years old and I'll associate with whomever I want to!'

'Oh, no, you won't!' retorted Philip with a mirthless laugh. 'If you want to try your strength of will against mine, Katarina, go ahead! But I warn you now—it's a contest you can only lose.'

Kate gasped with rage.

'You arrogant swine!' she cried. 'What right do you think you have to tell me who I can and can't associate with? It's nothing to do with you!'

'Oh, yes, it is!' said Philip hoarsely, and he caught her by the wrist and drew her hard against him.

Kate felt ready to swoon with longing at the feeling of those strong, imperious arms around her body, but she struggled spiritedly.

'Would you mind telling me why?' she demanded.

Philip's only response was to drag her against him even harder and subject her to a long, fierce kiss. His mouth was warm and passionate, and his hands moved over her body in an urgent, desperate rhythm as if he was impelled by a blind need to possess her.

'Because you are my woman,' he said huskily.

As suddenly as he had caught hold of her he released her. Kate gave a small, shaky sigh and looked up at him with eyes misted with tears.

'That's ridiculous, Philip,' she replied with a tremor in her voice. 'How can you say that when only last night you were ignoring me and making up to Irene as if she were the only woman on earth?'

Philip looked at her with disbelief in his eyes.

'Is that why you were dancing with Stavros last night?' he demanded savagely. 'Is that why you went off alone with him today?'

Kate pressed her lips firmly together, trying to stop them from quivering.

'Well, why shouldn't I?' she flared. 'Last night you made it only too plain that you didn't want anything further to do with me. I may be slow, Philip, but I'm not stupid. I realise now that you've been playing games with me ever since you met me, but when it's an official occasion you just don't want to know me, do you? As soon as I saw you putting that necklace around Irene's neck I realised that, whatever lies you might have told me, the two of you are really in love with each other. As far as you're capable of loving anyone. And you've just been using me.'

'Don't be so damned ridiculous!' retorted Philip. 'Presenting that necklace to Irene was just part of a ceremony that was planned months ago, before I even met you. As for my being in love with Irene, well, you saw for yourself on your first day here how little we enjoy each other's company. And, if you're worried about Irene sobbing her eyes out because I'm here with you tonight, well, save your pity. She flew out this morning to spend a week in Monte Carlo with Yves Sauvignon!'

Kate felt a curious lightening of her spirits at this news, but she stuck to her guns.

'That may be true,' she said suspiciously, 'but it doesn't explain the way you gave me the cold shoulder. I've never felt as humiliated in my life as I did last night when you snubbed me in front of everybody.'

'Humiliated?' demanded Philip incredulously. 'You felt humiliated?'

'Yes!' cried Kate. 'I can't believe the way you behaved in front of that reporter. "Oh, yes. Ho, ho, ho! This is Kate Walsh, one of my willing slaves, who I generously took out to lunch, but Kate is getting on her bike any day now and leaving, aren't you, sweetie?" Yes, as a matter of fact, I am, Philip. But, never mind, I'm sure you'll soon find another willing foreign girl who'll roll over and beg whenever you snap your fingers. One who's even more gullible than I am!'

'You little fool!' whispered Philip tenderly and he drew her back into his arms, where she promptly burst into tears.

She tried to pull away, but he stroked her hair soothingly and held her crushed against his chest so that she could hear the steady beating of his heart.

'I hate you!' she said in a muffled voice, which only caused him to put a finger under her chin and lift her tear-stained face to his.

'Do you?' he replied gravely. 'My poor love!'

But there was an unmistakable twitch of his lips as he spoke.

'I'm not your love, and it's nothing to laugh about!' retorted Kate furiously.

'Oh, Katarina, Katarina!' mourned Philip, playing with her wild auburn curls and kissing the ends of them. 'You say you were humiliated by my behaviour last night, but did you ever stop to think how much more humiliation you would have suffered if I had given those reporters the least hint of my true feelings towards you?'

'What do you mean?' demanded Kate, looking startled.

Philip's eyes were serious now as he looked into hers. He gritted his teeth and then spoke with suppressed passion.

'Supposing I had said "I love Katherine Walsh more than I have ever, ever loved another woman, and I have the gravest doubts as to whether I can bear to marry anybody else", what do you think would have happened?'

Kate was staring at him as if she were in a trance.

'It would be all over the papers tomorrow...' she said slowly.

'That or something far more lurid,' agreed Philip. 'Are you ready to cope with that, Katarina? Am I? Is Irene?'

'But is it true?' asked Kate in a dazed voice. 'Is that really what you feel about me, Philip?'

He was silent for a moment. Then his face contorted and he nodded.

'Heaven help me, Katarina!' he sighed. 'Yes, it is true.'

She moved into his arms like a sleepwalker, and he crushed her in a fierce, silent embrace. After a long, long moment they moved reluctantly apart.

'Then what are we going to do?' asked Kate.

Philip shook his head despairingly.

'I never thought I'd go against tradition and break an engagement,' he said half to himself. 'It doesn't seem like an honourable thing to do, but I suppose it's the only way. As soon as Irene comes back from Monte Carlo I'll talk to her about it.'

On the morning that Irene was due back from Monte Carlo, Kate awoke with a sinking sensation in the pit of her stomach. All week she had been swinging from elation to despair and back again. Just when she was convinced that Philip meant every word he had said to her, a small mocking voice inside her would whisper, 'It's just a trick to seduce you!' Remembering Leon Clark's deception, she clung fiercely to her resolve to keep Philip at a distance until she knew the truth. If Philip really did break off his engagement with Irene, then Kate would feel free to give full rein to her passion. Until then she was determined not even to let him touch her. It was a decision they both found difficult, and Kate longed for the waiting to be over.

Consequently, when the doorbell of her villa rang shortly before lunch on Sunday afternoon, she sprang to her feet and ran to open it. Philip stood smiling warmly at her, and her heart leapt.

'Have you spoken to Irene yet?' she asked.

He shook his head. 'I sent a car to meet her at the airport,' he said, 'but the driver couldn't find her, so I assume she must be catching a later plane. Don't look so disappointed, Katarina. She's bound to be here in another day or two, and then we'll get everything sorted out. And in the meantime, I've come to take you to lunch.'

'I'm not sure that I ought to have lunch alone with you, Philip. I mean, until you and Irene——'

'This has nothing to do with Irene,' said Philip impatiently. 'And, anyway, you won't be alone with me. In fact, I'm just the messenger boy. The invitation actually comes from the Vassiliou family. Anna told me when she arrived at work this morning that Nikos is due back from hospital today and Kyria Vassiliou wants us both to come to lunch. Particularly you.'

'Isn't that nice of them?' said Kate, overwhelmed. 'But are you sure I wouldn't be intruding?'

Philip gazed at her thoughtfully.

'Greeks very rarely invite outsiders to their homes,' he said. 'The home is very private, a meeting place only for family and the closest friends. They want to honour you by inviting you and they'll be very hurt if you don't come.'

'Then of course I'll come,' agreed Kate. 'Do you think it would be in order to bring my camera, Philip? Then I could take some photos of the family to give them later.'

'I think they'd be delighted,' said Philip. 'I'll pick you up about one o'clock.'

When Kate and Philip reached the village they made their way up to the Vassilious' house with an escort of dogs and children. The entire household was grouped on the terrace waiting to receive them. Nikos, looking rather pale and with his right arm in a sling, Anna, sporting a cheeky grin and for once minus her headphones, their older sister Eleni and her baby and, of course their parents, Kyria Vassiliou, a small grey-haired woman dressed in black and Kyrios Vassiliou, a dignified man whose brown eyes held the same mischievous twinkle as Anna's.

Time flew by, and Kate was overwhelmed by the hospitality of the family. After the disaster of her visit to the coffee house she had bought herself a book on Greek customs so that she was able to make a good impression on the family. When Eleni shyly handed over her baby to be admired, Kate cuddled the tiny bundle lovingly and stammered the appropriate good wishes in Greek.

'*Na sas zisi*. May he live for you. Ptt. Ptt. Ptt.'

As she completed the ritual pretence of spitting to drive away bad luck from the baby, there was a general murmur of astonishment and delight.

'Well done,' whispered Philip as they went into the dining-room. 'Everybody's thrilled with the way you're fitting in.'

The meal was delicious and the warmth and hospitality of the family were so overwhelming that Kate felt quite sorry when it was time to go home. On Philip's suggestion, they decided to walk back to the hotel along the scenic track which led along the cliff-tops. The late afternoon sun was slanting steeply through the trees as Philip led her down the hill to the point where the village gave way to vineyards and vegetable gardens. Together they plunged into a silvery, rippling sea of olive groves, and climbed another hill overlooking the water. At this point the cleared land ended and a track wound away through thick, aromatic green scrub.

'It's really dense and wild-looking, isn't it?' marvelled Kate.

'That's right,' agreed Philip. 'But it's no more than a kilometre or so to the hotel, and we'll get some really spectacular views of the sea. And I can show you where I'm planning to build the marina next summer.'

Kate fell into step beside him and trailed one hand through a glossy oleander bush, which still had a few faded pink blossoms clinging to it. Through the gaps in the shrubs she could see the sapphire-blue water of the Mediterranean down below.

'Greece is a photographer's paradise!' she exclaimed.
'I could stay here for half a dozen lifetimes and never
get tired of it.'

'Could you?' asked Philip in an odd voice. Then,
before she had a chance to answer, he went on talking.
'Speaking of photographers' paradises,' he said briskly,
'I've taken the liberty of sending your prints of the
windmills of Mykonos to a photographic agency in
Athens. The man who runs it, Tassos Astrinakis, is a
very fine photographer himself. He used to do some of
my travel brochures for my earlier hotels. But, like you,
he hankered after better things. These days he earns his
bread and butter doing high-quality greetings cards for
the tourists, and has an exhibition once a year of his
artistic photos. If he likes your work I'm sure he'll try
to help you.'

'That's very kind of you, Philip,' said Kate in a
troubled voice. She was touched by his efforts to help
her, but still uneasily conscious of a need to keep him
at arm's length. After all, he was still Irene's fiancé, not
hers. Should she really be accepting favours from him
like this?

'Well, I hate to see talent go to waste,' said Philip
casually. 'But now let's go and see my marina site.'

They padded along silently over the uneven ground.
In most places the track was wide enough for them to
walk abreast, but at times it narrowed so much that they
had to go in single file. Although there were no tall trees,
many of the shrubs had dense, bushy branches that tore
at Kate's clothes and the ground underfoot was rocky
and uneven. She had to tread carefully, and it was rather
a relief when Philip called a halt in a small clearing overlooking the sea.

'Look down there,' he commanded, pointing to the
north-west. 'See where that spit of land forms a natural
breakwater? That's where I'm going to build the marina.'

'Oh, yes,' said Kate, shading her eyes against the glare. 'Is that the *Eleftheria* moored down there at the moment?'

'Yes, it is,' agreed Philip.

He came a step closer to Kate and his hands rested lightly on her shoulders. His face was so close to hers that she could see each individual eyelash, the glint of desire in his brown eyes, the warm sensual curve of his mouth and the way his chest rose and fell as frantically as if he had been running a long, hard race.

'Don't, Philip!' she begged breathlessly, backing away from him. 'You know we agreed not to——!'

Her foot hit a low outcrop of rock and there was a shrill, protesting squawk from beneath it. Kate stopped in bewilderment.

'What was that?' she demanded.

'What was what?' asked Philip.

'That noise. Didn't you hear it? Listen, there it is again.' Crouching down on her heels, she peered under the outcrop of rock. 'Oh, Philip, look! The poor thing! It's a seagull, isn't it?'

Philip knelt down too, and looked in under the overhanging rock at the pathetic grey and white bird that was sheltering there. Its plumage was still glossy and beautiful on the wings and back, but the white breast-feathers were stained with blood and one leg dangled limply. Yet, in spite of this, the bird lowered its head and shrieked defiance at them.

'A stray cat or a dog from the village must have got it,' said Philip. 'Poor thing. It'll never survive with that broken leg.'

Kate's eyes filled with tears.

'What are we going to do?' she asked. 'We can't just leave it there to die. Can't we splint its leg or something?'

Philip shook his head compassionately.

'I don't think it's got a hope,' he said gently. 'See how the breast is torn too? The kindest thing we can do is to put it out of its misery. Look, Katarina, you go on down the track a bit and I'll deal with it. Take some photos or something, and I'll catch you up in a little while, OK?'

Kate's lip quivered, but she nodded. Deep down she knew Philip was right. Hastily averting her eyes as he picked up a rock, she hurried off down the track.

She had only gone another two hundred yards or so when a patch of purple heather halfway down the rugged hillside caught her attention. Against the dazzling blue water of the sea it made a stunning composition, and she unclipped her camera case, took off the lens cap and moved cautiously down towards it. Squinting into the viewfinder and tiptoeing around to locate the best angle, she was scarcely aware of the rest of her surroundings. She adjusted the focus ring very slowly and leant forward to take the shot.

'What the hell do you think you're doing?' demanded a furious voice.

Kate gasped as the camera was wrenched savagely out of her hands and flung to the ground. As her vision took in the wider view, she had the sudden appalled realisation of what had happened. A half-naked couple had been lying on a rug in the bushes only a few yards from her subject and she had disturbed them.

'I-I'm sorry!' she stammered. 'I didn't mean to intrude! I was just photographing the heather. I didn't even see—— Oh!'

For she had suddenly recognised the girl who was struggling to pull on her red bikini-top. It was Irene Marmara. Giving up the struggle as hopeless, Irene flung aside the flimsy scrap of material and wrapped a towel around herself. Then she scrambled to her feet and confronted Kate angrily.

'How dare you spy on Yves and me?' she demanded furiously. 'I'll have you fired for this!'

'I don't think so, Irene,' said a harsh voice.

They all gazed up the hillside to the track where Philip stood looking down at them. Kate saw Yves Sauvignon close his eyes for a moment and shudder. Then Philip sauntered down the hillside towards them. His gaze flickered contemptuously from Yves's brief swimming-trunks to Irene's discarded bikini-top, then came to rest on his fiancée's face.

'I think this farce has gone on long enough,' he said curtly. 'Irene, I must ask you to consider our engagement at an end.'

CHAPTER SIX

IN THE stunned silence which followed this announcement Kate heard the soft lap-lap of the waves at the foot of the cliffs, the hoarse braying of a donkey in the distance, the rapid uneven thudding of her own heart. Then Irene let rip with a torrent of invective in Greek. Flinging herself on Philip, she clawed at his face and pummelled his chest with her fists.

'You louse!' she shrieked. 'How dare you try and make me look a fool like this?'

'You're making yourself look a fool,' retorted Philip sharply.

Seizing her wrists, he held her at arm's length and glanced contemptuously at the towel which was slipping precariously off her shoulders.

'If you've quite finished your little sunbathing session with your lover, I suggest you get dressed,' he added scathingly.

Flinging him a venomous glance, Irene hastily pulled a T-shirt over her head.

'We *were* only sunbathing, you know, Andronikos,' put in Yves nervously.

Philip's gaze flickered incredulously over the younger man's tanned, youthful physique.

'You must think I'm a fool if you suppose that I'll believe that,' said Philip harshly. 'And, even if it were true, I would not want my future wife sunbathing half-naked with another man. But you can spare me your lies. I'm well aware that you and Irene have been lovers for several weeks now.'

'Well, what if we have?' demanded Irene defiantly. 'You've never spent any time with me. You're always too busy slaving away in your office, trying to impress people with how important you are. And you never want me to have any fun or go anywhere or do anything. At least Yves is good company, which is more than I can say for you!'

'Then you should be delighted that you're no longer faced with marrying me,' retorted Philip in a dangerous voice.

Irene paled.

'That wasn't what I meant!' she exclaimed. 'All right, Philip, so I had a bit of fun with Yves, but what does it matter? I've never interfered with your pleasures! No doubt you've been sleeping with that little slut of a photographer ever since she arrived here, but I've bitten my tongue and looked the other way. And, if you want to keep seeing her, I'll do the same thing after we're married.'

'You're not listening, Irene,' said Philip in a hard voice. 'We aren't getting married.'

He turned away, but Irene caught his arm.

'That's ridiculous!' she cried. 'This engagement was arranged when I was a child.'

'I know,' agreed Philip bitterly. 'Perhaps that's why it's been such a dismal failure. If we'd had our choice as free adults I don't think either of us would have chosen each other. You think I'm stern and humourless and a killjoy, and I think you're a selfish, frivolous brat. Face it, Irene: we're well rid of each other!'

'No!' screamed Irene. 'Philip, you can't humiliate me like this in front of the entire village.'

Philip sighed wearily.

'What's the village got to do with it?' he demanded. 'You don't have to tell them I broke the engagement. Say you did it yourself. Tell them you wanted to marry Yves instead.' He cast the Frenchman a swift malicious glance. Yves shifted uncomfortably.

'Now just a minute——' he began.

But Irene pushed him impatiently aside, still keeping her hold on Philip's arm.

'I'm not interested in marrying Yves!' she cried. 'Philip, listen to me! You can't just push me aside because of a meaningless affair. That has nothing to do with our marriage. We've been promised to each other for years—it was a business arrangement!'

Philip looked down at her with an expression that held more pity than anger.

'That's just it,' he replied. 'I no longer want a marriage that is only a business arrangement. When I marry I intend to marry for love, Irene. Now stand out of my way!'

With an impatient sigh he shook her off. Losing her grip on his sleeve, Irene staggered back and looked wildly about. Her gaze settled on Kate and she gave an angry sob.

'You little bitch! This is all your fault!' she cried.

And, running at Kate, she gave her a violent push. Kate gasped, but Philip's arms came round her like hoops of steel as he steadied her on her feet.

'You slut!' panted Irene. 'I'll go to the papers about this. I'll drag your name through the mud. You'll wish you'd never crossed me, you pathetic little nobody!'

'Irene!'

Philip's voice was like a whiplash.

'If you ever do anything to tarnish Kate's good name I'll make you wish you'd never been born!' he promised. 'Do I make myself clear?'

'Oh, very clear,' seethed Irene contemptuously. 'She's just what you deserve, you peasant! You never had anything until my father took you on and supported you. You owe everything you've got to the Marmaras!'

'On the contrary, Irene,' said Philip through his teeth, 'you owe practically everything you've got to me. But I'm not prepared to argue with you about it. I wish you and Yves joy of your new life! Come, Katarina.'

He took Kate's arm and hurried her up the hillside towards the path. Irene's voice floated after them.

'You won't get away with this!' she howled. 'Do you hear me, Philip Andronikos? I'll ruin you. You'll pay for what you've done to me. Both of you!'

Kate gave a small shaky sigh as the welcome shrubbery closed round them again.

'Are you all right?' asked Philip, glancing down at her.

'Yes, I'm fine,' agreed Kate, pressing one hand to her rapidly thudding heart. 'Just a bit shaken up. Oh, but Philip, she's scratched your face!'

She put one hand up to his cheek, but found her fingers caught and held.

'I think I'll live,' said Philip with a laugh. 'And I doubt if she's even spoiled my beauty. So let's get back to my house, shall we? I think we've got things to discuss.'

He kissed Kate's fingertips, then caught her hand in his. All the way down the track he hummed a Greek melody under his breath. The same wild, rousing song he had played on the bouzouki the first time they had met. Kate looked at him in perplexity.

'Are you sure you're all right?' she insisted.

'Better than all right,' replied Philip. 'Intoxicated is more like it.'

The path took a sharp twist, revealing a villa half hidden by rambling gardens on a hillside overlooking the sea. There was a high stone fence inset with wrought-iron railings and a garden dominated by pines and cypresses. Philip opened a small metal gate to one side of the main driveway and led Kate down a gravel path flanked by flowering plants. Somewhere a fountain was splashing musically into a pool, and lizards darted away at their approach. Then a curve in the path revealed a large whitewashed house, covered in blazing scarlet bougainvillaea. Philip took a key from his pocket and unlocked the heavy, carved front door.

'I don't think you've been in my house before, have you?' he asked casually.

He flung open the door and ushered Kate inside. She paused for a moment, dazzled by the sudden coolness and dimness. Then her eyes grew used to the change in brightness and she looked round her. She was in a spacious hallway with doors opening on either side and a huge marble staircase curving away out of sight to the floor above. Overhead hung a vast chandelier, which caught the light from the central stairwell and gave it back in a hundred refracted rainbows. The walls contained recessed niches, each of which held a beautiful piece of art. A Chinese jade statue, a porcelain jug, an ancient Greek vase.

'Oh, Philip, it's beautiful,' she breathed.

Philip shrugged.

'Recently I'd begun to think that it was rather like my life,' he said thoughtfully. 'Glamorous, full of expensive possessions and completely empty. But then I met you.'

He was gazing down at her now with a hungry, yearning expression and, like a sleepwalker, she moved into his arms.

'Oh, Philip,' she whispered.

He caught her against him so fiercely that she cried out, then he turned her face up to his and kissed her. A long, bruising kiss that seemed to make her bones turn to water so that she could hardly stand when he released her.

'Will you marry me?' he asked abruptly.

'W-what?' she exclaimed, taken aback by the suddenness of it all. 'Philip, have you gone crazy?'

He laughed. A joyful, ringing laugh that made the staircase echo.

'No,' he retorted gladly. 'Quite the reverse. I've just gone completely sane and stopped caring about things that don't matter a damn, like money and property and tradition. I don't want any of that, Katarina. I just want you.'

'Are you sure?' asked Kate huskily.

'Surer than I've ever been of anything in my life,' said Philip firmly. 'Now, will you marry me or not?'

He gave her a small, impatient shake and she found herself halfway between tears and laughter.

'But, Philip, you're rich and well known!' she cried. 'And I'm nobody! And you've only known me for a few weeks. How can you possibly want to marry me?'

'Katarina,' he said urgently, 'the reason I've succeeded in life is because I've always known exactly what I've wanted and gone after it. And I want you. What's more, I'm not even asking you to marry me any more. I'm telling you. You've got to marry me! Is that clear?'

His eyes smouldered, his chin jutted forward and his body took on a fierce, determined stance, as if he were going into battle. Kate gave a small, gasping laugh, then beat on his shoulders with her fists.

'Yes,' she wailed. 'Yes, Philip. That's clear!'

His gaze softened and he looked down at her with an intense yearning hunger that made her quiver with desire.

'You don't have any objections, do you?' he asked.

She caught her lower lip in her teeth and shook her head wordlessly. With a sudden sharp intake of breath Philip lifted her bodily off the floor and ran for the stairs.

'Philip, put me down! Stop! Where are you taking me?'

He paused on the landing to plant a swift, burning kiss on her lips.

'You know where I'm taking you!' he replied throatily. 'And don't pretend you don't want it too, Katarina. Your body betrays you!'

He glanced down at the flimsy material of her bodice, where his strong brown hand caressed the swelling mound of her breast. She saw that her nipple was a hard, urgent peak against the thin fabric, and her face flamed. A tiny gasping moan escaped her.

'Don't fight it, my darling,' urged Philip exultantly. 'I want to enjoy every inch of your beautiful, precious body.'

He kicked open a door and carried her into a room more lavish than she had ever seen before. In a daze, Kate noticed magnificent wall tapestries, carved antique furniture, a large gilt mirror that caught the light from the windows and filled the room with radiance. Then Philip set her down in the middle of an enormous four-poster bed and she no longer noticed anything but him. His eyes were dark and dilated with passion, and his breath came in a sharp uneven rhythm as he stared down at her. One powerful hand touched the velvety softness of her cheek and then trailed slowly and ecstatically down over the swelling curves of her body. Kate let out a tiny moan of delight and felt herself shudder beneath his touch.

'You are beautiful, *agapimou*,' breathed Philip. 'And you are mine. All mine!'

With suppressed violence he began to tear off his shirt and trousers, wrenching at buttons and fastenings, so that Kate heard the sharp ripping sound of torn fabric. Then he flung away his clothes and stood before her, totally naked. A tremor ran through Kate and she stared at him, transfixed. His body was beautifully proportioned, with lean, powerful muscles and an amazing quality of animal magnetism. Dark springy hair covered his chest and ran in a thin line below his navel. As he moved towards her she saw the rippling interplay of muscles below his skin, and a throbbing tide of desire flooded through her.

'Your turn now,' he whispered, setting his lips to her throat so that his breath tickled her. 'I want to stroke and caress every part of you, Katarina. I want you to ache and shiver and burn with longing for me, just as I do for you.'

Some primitive instinct of shyness made her struggle for an instant as his hands touched her breasts. But he bore her down with the full, urgent weight of his body, holding her pinned beneath him with one powerful hand, while the other unbuttoned her blouse. It was a task he performed wantonly, caressingly, delighting in the blush that coloured her cheeks. But, before he was finished, impatience overtook him and he wrenched open the last three buttons, exposing her naked skin to his gaze. She tried to hide her face against his chest, pressing herself against his rough hair and breathing in the spicy masculine scent of him, but he would have none of that. With barely controlled force he thrust her back against the pillows and gazed down at her exultantly.

'I want to look at you,' he growled softly. 'I want to feast my eyes on your auburn curls, your creamy white skin, your little rosebud nipples, your round, strong hips...'

As he spoke he was slipping her clothes expertly off her body, unsnapping her bra, teasing the sleeves of her blouse down over her arms, rolling her skirt sensually down over her thighs. And, as he undressed her, he pressed kisses on her freshly exposed skin. Kate felt as if a trail of fire were licking down her body and then blazing furiously out of control. She arched her back and gasped, clutching at his springy dark curls as his warm lips moved across the satiny surface of her thigh and trying to draw his head up so that she could kiss him. But he thrust her back down with a swift, commanding gesture.

'Later, *agapimou*,' he said softly. 'I will teach you what pleases me. But first you must have some pleasure of your own. Now lie still and let me feast on you.'

She gave herself up to enjoyment then, writhing and gasping with delight as Philip's mouth and hands found the most sensitive spots and brought her an ecstasy that was close to torment. Her own excitement was mounting unbearably and she shifted protestingly against him, uttering cries of passion. Only when she was moaning and quivering uncontrollably beneath his touch did Philip allow her to take any active part herself.

'Are you ready, my darling?' he whispered.

Her eyes were closed and she could feel her lips set in a shuddering grimace of longing, but she nodded, reaching out blindly to touch his face and run her hands over his shoulders.

'Then stroke me,' he urged. 'Let me feel your long, slender fingers all over my body.'

Her eyelids fluttered open and she saw the flare of desire in his face. Then, with a small, purring laugh, she knelt beside him and set to work to inflict the same delicious torment on him. Hesitantly at first, and then with growing boldness, she caressed his body, her mouth lingering against the rough dark hair on his chest, while her hand trailed lower and lower in tantalising circles across his skin. She felt him tense and groan, then he caught her against him with a strength that was savage in its intensity.

'I love you, Katarina,' he cried. 'And I want to take you as my wife!'

Burying his face in the tumbled fragrance of her hair, he flung himself ruthlessly on top of her. She gave a small, whimpering cry as the links of his gold neck-chain bit into her tender flesh, but he stilled her protest with a kiss that made her gasp with longing. Fire seemed to leap and quiver through her veins as his mouth claimed hers, and she sank back into the pillows, wordlessly inviting him to possess her. When the moment came she was beyond speech, beyond anything but a deep, primitive groundswell of emotion that swept her along like a tidal wave. Dimly she was aware of the weight and strength and warmth of his body on top of hers, of the tiny murmuring cries that escaped her, of the powerful rhythmic force that drove them along together. But all sense of her own identity seemed to be lost as she clung to him in a throbbing ecstasy of passion until the final crescendo.

She felt his fingers tighten in her hair, heard him hoarsely cry out her name, then the universe exploded around her with the dark, pulsating heat of total fulfilment. Slowly she came back to earth to find her body limp and exhausted in his hold. Putting up one hand, she pushed her damp, sticky curls away from her forehead and then put her arm tentatively around his neck. His hand came up and closed on hers, and they remained for a moment in silence, locked together in the warm aftermath of passion. Then, with a low murmur of well-being, Philip raised his head and looked down at her.

'Did I ever tell you that I loved you?' he asked tenderly.

'Mmm, but you can tell me again,' crooned Kate, snuggling up to him as he slid down on to the bed beside her.

Obligingly he took her fingertips and kissed them one by one.

'I love you, Katarina,' he said after each kiss.

She giggled and nestled into the hollow of his shoulder.

'Oh, Philip,' she sighed, 'I never imagined there could be anything as wonderful as this. Do you know that you are perfect? Absolutely perfect!'

'Yes, I've often thought so,' agreed Philip modestly. 'But it's nice to hear you say it.'

'You conceited beast!' cried Kate, springing to her knees and snatching up a pillow. 'How dare you make fun of me?'

Raising the pillow, she brought it down forcefully on his head, but as she raised her arms for a second assault Philip caught the pillow and flung it away. Holding her pinioned by the wrists, he gazed admiringly up at her body.

'You know, that does the most wonderful thing to your breasts,' he said appreciatively. 'I think I'll get you to kneel like that more often.'

A slow warmth crept into Kate's cheeks.

'Stop it, Philip,' she protested, wriggling a little and hanging her head.

He laughed. A rich, reverberating laugh full of vitality and joy.

'I think you'd better get used to me looking at your body,' he teased. 'I intend to do a lot of it in future. And not just looking either.'

Gently he guided her arms back down to her sides, but as he did so he leant forward and brushed her nipples with his lips. A tremor went through Kate's body and she heard Philip give a faint groan. Rising to his feet, he picked up his dressing-gown, which was lying over a chair.

'The things you do to me!' he lamented. 'By my reckoning, it's approximately two minutes since I finished making love to you and already you're filling me with unmentionable thoughts. Perhaps a decent interval for refreshments would be a good idea. Do you want some tea?'

'Yes, please,' agreed Kate, nestling back into the pillows and pulling the covers self-consciously up to her shoulders.

When Philip arrived back five minutes later with a tea-tray, she was lying blissfully with her eyes closed and her glorious auburn hair blazing like a halo against the pillows. Philip chuckled.

'You look radiant,' he murmured. 'As if you had just arrived in paradise.'

'I feel as if I had!' she retorted, stretching herself sensually. 'But I suppose I'll have to come down to earth some time. Where are my clothes?' She sat up and looked around her rather helplessly.

'You could have your tea in bed,' suggested Philip.

Kate shook her head.

'No, there are biscuits,' she objected. 'I hate crumbs in the bed. I'll get up and get dressed.'

Wordlessly Philip held up her blouse in one hand and three loose buttons in the other. 'Are you sure?' he asked in a deadpan voice.

Kate choked on a protesting laugh. 'Philip, you—you caveman!' she cried.

'I'll buy you another one,' he promised. 'In the meantime I can offer you a spare dressing-gown.'

The dressing-gown which he took out of the huge carved wardrobe was made out of a decidedly masculine plaid, and so large that Kate almost swam in it. Sighing, she folded back the sleeves.

'How do I look?' she demanded, doing a grotesque pirouette.

'Awful,' said Philip frankly. 'I'm sorry I don't have anything more feminine to offer you.'

'I'm glad you don't,' retorted Kate with spirit. 'I wouldn't really like to think of you having a wardrobe full of lace négligés waiting for the queue of women you entice into your bed.'

Philip ruffled her hair and dropped a swift kiss on it.

'There will only ever be you, Katarina,' he promised. 'Now come and pour the tea.'

Once she had a cup of fragrant lemon-scented tea and a raspberry-cream biscuit in front of her, Kate looked at Philip with a troubled smile.

'Philip,' she said bluntly, 'what do you think Irene meant when she threatened to ruin us? Could she really do that?'

Philip shook his head in exasperation and smiled back at her, his gaze resting warmly on her tumbled curls and flushed cheeks. Reaching across, he took her hand and planted a kiss on the inside of her wrist.

'I don't think she meant anything at all by it,' he replied firmly, 'except that she hates to be thwarted. Once she calms down she'll realise that breaking the engagement was the best thing for both of us. We would never have been happy together. So don't worry your head about it for another minute. You and I have much pleasanter matters to discuss.'

'Such as?' prompted Kate, smiling shyly.

'How about our marriage plans for a start?' suggested Philip. 'Or a nice, sun-soaked cruise on the *Eleftheria*? Or the fifteen children we're going to have when we get back from the cruise?'

Kate choked with laughter.

'I do love you, Philip!' she exclaimed. 'But fifteen!'

'Well, two or three,' he amended. 'Once your career's established. But first the wedding. When do you want to get married?'

'As soon as possible!' retorted Kate promptly, helping herself to another biscuit.

'My sentiments exactly,' agreed Philip with satisfaction. 'I'll see Father Stargos about it. There's only two things, though, Katarina—would you mind if we had a very quiet wedding? Just a simple ceremony in the village with your parents and a few of my closest friends?'

'Whatever you want,' murmured Kate.

Philip gave a sigh of relief.

'Good!' he said. 'And there's the other thing: could I ask you not to mention our engagement to any outsiders? You can write to your family, of course, but I'd rather keep it quiet apart from that.'

'You're not having second thoughts, are you?' asked Kate in a troubled voice.

'No, of course not!' exclaimed Philip impatiently. 'But you know how I hate reporters, Katarina. Ever since I really got into the big league with my hotels they've been swarming around underfoot wherever I go. And my break-up with Irene is going to be just the sort of juicy gossip they thrive on. You can't imagine how obnoxious they can be, and I don't want you subjected to all that pressure. And I particularly don't want our wedding turned into a media circus. So I think secrecy's our best option. Agreed?'

'I suppose you're right,' admitted Kate. 'But I would have liked to tell my friends at the dig. Oh, well, never mind. Tell me more about this cruise you're planning.'

Philip's eyes kindled.

'Well, I haven't had a holiday for over five years,' he said. 'And the *Eleftheria's* just sitting idle at anchor. Now that the hotel opening is over I think you and I should just make a break for it. Dorothea and the others can run the hotel with their eyes closed, so why don't we just sail off into the Mediterranean and treat ourselves to a good time? Snorkelling, sunbathing, fishing, cruising around the islands—how does that sound?'

'It sounds wonderful,' agreed Kate longingly. 'But do you really think you should leave right now, Philip? I mean, you did say that your backer Hristos Hionides had suffered a heart attack and there could be trouble over the mortgage if he died. Shouldn't you stay here to deal with it all?'

Philip winced.

'I know,' he admitted, flinging up his hands. 'But really it's very unlikely that Hristos will die or that his executors will make any trouble for me if he does. And, if I wait for that problem to be resolved, something else is sure to crop up. There will always be something demanding my attention, Katarina. If I don't seize the chance for happiness while it's here it may slip out of my grasp completely. For years I've done nothing but work and worry. Now that I've got you I want to live a little too. Is that such a bad thing?'

Kate looked at him steadily. Outside the window the light was beginning to fade, and the table-lamp threw his features into sharp relief. She saw with concern that there were shadows under his eyes and lines of strain etched around the corners of his mouth.

'No,' she said softly. 'Philip, you look exhausted. Why don't you go back to bed and rest? I'm sure you didn't sleep at all last night.'

'I didn't really,' he admitted. 'All right, Katarina. I'll go to sleep now on one condition.'

'Oh?' she said questioningly.

'That you come with me,' he insisted, ruffling her hair. 'We'll have some dinner sent over later from the hotel, and tomorrow we'll hit the high seas!'

Kate struggled out of a fog of sleep a few hours later to the sound of the insistent shrilling of a bell.

'Mmm. What is it?' she grumbled protestingly.

Philip dropped a swift, light kiss on her hair.

'Just our dinner,' he reassured her. 'That's the back doorbell. I'll go down and fetch it.'

He was back within five minutes with a tray of delicious food. Pitta bread, smoking hot and with a faint aroma of charcoal, a selection of vegetable and seafood dips, shish kebabs with fried potatoes and a salad of olives, tomatoes and cucumber, and small rich cakes called *cariocas* that tasted like velvety chocolate fudge. And, of course, a bottle of dark red Mavrodafni wine to wash it all down. They ate slowly, sensuously, feeding each other titbits and sharing a wine glass. Afterwards Philip took out his bouzouki and played a series of haunting love-songs. And when at last he set aside the instrument, they moved into each other's arms, driven by instincts older than words. Kate's last conscious feeling before she slipped away into sleep was a silent sense of wonder. I've never been so happy in my life as I am at this moment...

*   *   *

She woke hours later to the same insistent shrilling of a bell that had disturbed her the night before. Yawning, she sat up and pushed the hair out of her eyes.

'Philip?' she said.

But the bed was empty. The bell kept ringing insistently and Kate squinted at the clock on the bedside table. Seven thirty-four.

'I suppose that's our breakfast,' she said with resignation.

Hauling on Philip's oversized dressing-gown and slipping her feet into his thongs, she made her way towards the source of the sound. As she came down the marble staircase she heard the noise of running water in the downstairs bathroom. Well, that solved one mystery. Philip was obviously taking a shower. Wrapping her gown more tightly around her, she found her way hesitantly through to the kitchen and steeled herself to deal with one of the kitchen staff from the hotel. This could be embarrassing, she thought as she opened the door.

It was far more embarrassing than she could ever have imagined in her worst nightmare. For the man standing outside the kitchen door was not a hotel waiter, but a photographer. And the moment Kate opened the door he leapt inside, with his flashbulb exploding furiously. Kate recoiled with a cry of shock, and held on to the kitchen counter to steady herself.

'Is it true that you're Philip Andronikos's new mistress?' demanded the photographer. 'Did he throw over Irene Marmara for you? Were you a call-girl in Marseilles before you came to Áyios Dimitrios? Just turn your head, sweetie. I want a shot of that profile.'

Kate recovered herself slightly.

'How dare you?' she cried. 'Get out of here at once! Will you please leave?'

Flinging herself at him, she managed to send him careering back almost to the doorstep. But with practised ease he stuck his foot in the door and kept shooting.

'Ooh, that's great, baby! You look terrific in a rage like that! Now this time I want a full frontal. Not the rolling-pin, honey, you'll smash my lens. Did you really start out in pornographic movies?'

With an inarticulate cry of rage and dismay Kate gave up trying to get rid of the photographer and ran to the internal door of the kitchen.

'Philip! Philip!' she shrieked, clutching at the door-jamb.

A moment later Philip came racing down the hall, hastily wrapping a towel around his waist. His shoulders were beaded with moisture and his hair was dripping, but he took in the scene at a single glance. His face darkened and, thrusting Kate aside, he stepped forward and lifted the photographer right off his feet with a punch that sent him reeling on the floor. Then, lifting him up by the twisted lapels of his jacket, he flung him backwards out of the kitchen door. A moment later he ripped the film out of the camera, then threw the equipment contemptuously after its owner. Kate caught a brief glimpse of the photographer lying stupefied in the gravel, fingering his jaw, then Philip slammed the outer door.

'Damn!' he said. 'The vultures have already moved in. Well, we're going to have to get out of here, Katarina. I'm afraid he'll just be the first of many.'

Striding across to the telephone, he punched in a couple of numbers and spoke rapidly in Greek. When he put down the receiver he frowned thoughtfully.

'Right,' he said briskly, 'I've spoken to hotel security and asked them to escort our intruder off the premises, but, from the sound of things, there are more of them lurking around. And it's not easy to police eight-hundred acres, so you and I are getting out of here. Giorgos will collect us from my private jetty in the speedboat. Can you be dressed and ready in ten minutes?'

'Y-yes,' stammered Kate. 'But I've only got the clothes I came in last night. Everything else is over at my villa. Except for my camera.'

'Don't worry about it,' said Philip curtly. 'We'll sort it out once we're aboard the *Eleftheria*.'

Somehow Kate managed to shower and dress in the allotted ten minutes, and she was waiting in the hall with her camera and handbag when Philip came downstairs. He was dressed in navy trousers, a white and navy striped nautical shirt and rope-soled shoes, and he looked as casual and unperturbed as if this were nothing more than a normal outing. But Kate felt as if her insides were tied in knots of tension and fear. As they walked down the gravel path towards the jetty she kept darting quick, anxious glances around her as if an ambush of photographers might leap out of hiding at any moment. And, even when they were in the speedboat, flying across the blue water amid a shower of spray, she could not quite get rid of her apprehension. Only when they were aboard the yacht and she felt its powerful engines throb into life did some of her anxiety ebb away. With an understanding smile Philip led her into the saloon and motioned her into an armchair.

'Like something to drink?' he asked.

'Just some orange juice, thanks,' she said.

He handed her a tall glass, beaded with moisture.

'Cheers!' he murmured, clinking his own glass against hers. 'Now come on, smile. You're not going to let the vultures defeat you at the first encounter, are you?'

Kate gave a tremulous grin.

'Oh, Philip, that man was so horrible!' she exclaimed. 'He said such dreadful things about me and none of it was true. You don't really think all that stuff will appear in the media, do you?'

'Well, if it does, we won't be taking any notice of it,' said Philip firmly. 'I'll tell Giorgos that he's only to use the radio for weather forecasts. And, apart from that, we're going to stay strictly incommunicado for five or six days. We'll just go to one of the islands and forget that the rest of the world exists. How does that sound?'

'It sounds utterly blissful,' agreed Kate wistfully.

It was blissful. The weather was perfect, and the yacht's powerful engines sent it skimming over the water like a bird. Philip told Giorgos to set a course for the island of Thásos, and when they reached it they anchored in a quiet cove to the east of Mount Ypsari. They spent the days sunbathing, or snorkelling in the vivid blue waters, and at night they sat out on the deck, gazing at the stars. There were meals at the little tavernas in the port of Potamia Skala and invigorating runs along the beach at Khrysoammoudio. And on one memorable occasion they simply stayed in bed all day, emerging at nightfall only for a bathe in the jacuzzi, followed by a lavish dinner.

Kate used roll after roll of film, trying to capture the sparkle of the royal blue water, the dazzling white houses, the play of the light on the landscape. And of course there were photos of her and Philip too. Philip in fins and bathing-suit, sitting on the gunwale of the yacht, with his mask and snorkel pushed up over his wet curly hair and his white teeth gleaming. Photos of her, lying on a towel in a jade-green bikini with her nose bright with zinc cream and a lurid paperback open in her hands. There was even one daring photo of the two of them in the jacuzzi, both topless, and sensually embracing each other among the swirling bubbles.

'What on earth are you going to do with all these photos?' asked Philip as she set the automatic timer mechanism on her camera and slipped into the water beside him.

'Well, we could use them for advertising,' she suggested teasingly, winding her arms around his neck and smiling brilliantly as the camera flashed.

'Not this one!' retorted Philip, caressing her bare nipples with his fingertips. 'This one is strictly for private viewing only.'

'Mmm. Oh, Philip, that feels wonderful. I wish this holiday would never end!'

But it did end, of course. On the fifth day in Thásos they woke to find rain pattering dismally on the deck and grey scarves of cloud trailing in the sky overhead.

'What do you think?' asked Philip, turning up the collar of his yellow rain-slicker. 'Home?'

'Home,' confirmed Kate gloomily. 'Back to the paparazzi and Irene out after my blood.'

'Don't worry,' said Philip, dropping a lingering kiss on her damp curls. 'Things are sure to have improved by the time we get back.'

But they hadn't. When they finally came ashore at Áyios Dimitrios there was somebody waiting for them in the shelter of a large umbrella on the jetty. Kate's heart skipped a beat as she recognised Dorothea Zografou. But what on earth could be so urgent that it would make the deputy manager stand out in the pouring rain to meet them? Philip must have been thinking the same thing, for he was out of the speedboat before Giorgos had even finished making it fast to the jetty. Kate scrambled up the steps after him and saw that Dorothea had handed him a folded newspaper with large black headlines on the front page.

Stepping hesitantly between them, Kate looked down at the paper which was clutched in Philip's tense brown hands. The name Andronikos leapt out at her, but her Greek was not good enough to make out the rest.

'What does it say?' she demanded.

Philip's face was like a stone mask. He stared at the newspaper in disbelief, then tore it violently into halves and then quarters. Finally he walked across the jetty and flung it into a rubbish bin. Kate clutched his arm and shook him.

'What does it say?' she insisted.

Philip started slightly as if he were coming out of a trance. Then he passed one hand over his eyes, wiping away the rain that blurred his vision.

'It says "ANDRONIKOS FACES RUIN",' he replied grimly.

CHAPTER SEVEN

'WELL, come on,' said Dorothea practically. 'There's no sense standing around in the rain any longer. I just wanted to make sure I caught you before you disappeared to your own house. But what we need now is some action.'

Philip sighed and nodded.

'Have you got all the information I'll need?' he asked wearily.

'Up at my house,' agreed Dorothea with a flourish of her umbrella. 'Come on.'

Five minutes later they were sitting in Dorothea's living-room. Her house was a new one, built as part of the hotel complex and situated conveniently close to the main reception building. But it had the traditional features common to all the Hotel Ariadne buildings, and Kate found it difficult to believe that she wasn't cosily holed up in some remote mountain village. A fire crackled in the grate, woven rugs in shades of black and burgundy glowed against the whitewashed walls and a dull gold icon of the Virgin Mary hung in pride of place on one wall. But there was nothing cosy about the newspapers which lay scattered across the carved wooden dining table. Two or three of them were in English, and their headlines leapt out ominously at Kate.

'HEIRESS JILTS GREEK PLAYBOY!'
'ANDRONIKOS ON THE ROCKS?'
'LOVE AND RUIN FOR GREEK HOTEL DEVELOPER'

'What is this nonsense all about?' demanded Philip irritably, gesturing at the offending pile of papers.

'It sounds as if it's more than just nonsense, unfortunately,' retorted Dorothea. 'But take your wet things off first, Philip, and then I'll tell you what's been happening while you've been gone.'

Dorothea whisked away their wet rain-slickers, only to return a moment later with towels and a tray containing ouzo and three glasses. While they dried their hair she poured out three generous tots of the clear, sticky liquid.

'Yasas!' she said, lifting her glass.

'Ya!' they replied.

Kate choked as the fiery aniseed liqueur ran down her throat, but Dorothea and Philip looked as indifferent as if they were drinking water.

'Well, what's it all about?' demanded Philip.

Dorothea sighed.

'There are two separate stories,' she said succinctly. 'The first one is that Hristos Hionides has died and now his executors are threatening to call in the mortgages.'

Philip said nothing, but his hand tightened convulsively over his glass. Without knowing why, Kate felt a sudden chill of dismay run through her body.

'What does that mean?' she demanded.

'It means that I'll have to find a new financial backer for the hotel or I may go bankrupt,' replied Philip icily, his gaze still trained on Dorothea's face. 'But never mind that now. What's the other story that the papers are running, Dorothea?'

Dorothea winced.

'Without wanting to sound melodramatic,' she murmured, 'I'd say it's Irene's revenge. I don't know exactly what did happen after you left the village last week, but Irene's story is certainly a vivid one, and she's spread it around every second-rate newspaper and magazine in Europe. According to her, she came to your house unexpectedly, found you in bed with an Australian actress who stars in pornographic movies and promptly broke off her engagement to you.'

Philip made a strangled sound somewhere between a laugh and a groan.

'How could she be so spiteful?' he protested. 'It's ridiculous! Outrageous!'

An icy feeling of shock and dismay ran through Kate, and she felt her legs suddenly buckle beneath her. With a low gasp, she sank into a chair.

'Kate!' cried Philip. 'Don't take it so much to heart. Nobody believes the stuff they print in those dreadful rags!'

Her face was ashen pale, and he crouched beside her and chafed her cold fingers.

'Get her some more ouzo, Dorothea!' he ordered with a swift glance over his shoulder.

Dorothea came back immediately with a full glass, but by now Kate's hands were shaking so much that she couldn't keep a grip on it.

'I just can't believe anybody would say such awful things about me!' she said through chattering teeth.

'Ssshh. Now, now,' murmured Philip, holding the glass to her lips. 'It's not the end of the world, you know. And it's only because you're such an innocent that it shocks you so much. You should read some of the things they've written about me in the past! But the only thing to do is ignore it. The journalists will have their claws into somebody else by next week. What really worries me is this stuff about Hionides. Are you sure the report about his death is true, Dorothea?'

Dorothea nodded. 'I can't vouch for the statements about the mortgages, though,' she said. 'His solicitors refused to speak to me on the phone.'

Philip's lips met in a grim line.

'Then I'd better telephone them myself,' he said.

He paused to caress Kate's cold cheeks and smooth her damp curls back from her face.

'Will you be all right if I go and make a phone call?' he asked.

'Yes,' said Kate through frozen lips.

Dorothea ushered Philip out of the room and Kate was left alone to brood. She felt as shaken as if somebody she loved had just died. How on earth could she ever go out in public again if people were saying such dreadful things about her? But after a few moments she stopped thinking about herself and thought about the other half of Dorothea's news. What would it mean for Philip if the mortgages really were called in? Hadn't he said something about going bankrupt? She must get control of herself, try to offer him some support. But when the door opened again and she saw his face she could not banish the tremor from her voice.

'Is it true, then?' she asked in dismay.

'Yes!' he snapped. 'The executors to the will have foreclosed on the mortgages.'

His face looked as if it had been carved out of solid granite, with his features set in lines of pure fury and his dark eyes glittering with determination. Kate felt a tremor of fear resonate through her. She was only glad that Philip's rage was not directed against her.

'But why did they do it?' she demanded in bewilderment.

'Goodness knows,' retorted Philip, 'unless Hristos's heirs have decided they'll try and send me bankrupt so that they can buy the Hotel Ariadne for a song. But if that's their game I'll make them wish they'd never tried it! Dorothea, tell Yannis I want a car ready in half an hour.'

'W-where are you going?' stammered Kate.

'To Thessaloníki,' replied Philip. 'I need to see my lawyers and accountants. If I don't find another financial backer within the next two weeks I can kiss the Hotel Ariadne goodbye!'

Kate stared at him, aghast.

'But that means——'

'It means the end of everything I've spent my life working for!' he agreed savagely.

Then to Kate's astonishment he suddenly laughed.

'Except that it won't come to that!' he vowed. 'I've outwitted people who've tried to ruin me in business before, and I dare say I'll do it again. Come on, Katarina! Stop moping around like a pile of wet rags and come and help me pack!'

Half laughing, half crying, Kate found herself dragged out of Dorothea's house and up the path towards Philip's own villa.

'You know, you baffle me, Philip,' she complained as they crunched through the wet gravel to the huge front door.

'Oh, in what way?' demanded Philip, turning the key in the lock.

'Well, look at you!' replied Kate, propelling him across to the enormous gilt mirror that hung on one wall. 'Everything is going wrong all around you and yet you've got a spring in your step, your voice sounds lively and cheerful and you were actually whistling as we came up the driveway. Anyone would think you were enjoying yourself!'

Philip threw back his head and laughed. A rich, resonant sound. Then his hand reached out and touched her cheek. His eyes kindled as he looked at her.

'Do you know, I think I am?' he said softly. 'There's nothing I like better than a good fight, and what could be more worth fighting for than this? The woman I want to marry and the home I want to live in?'

He drew back the hood of her yellow oilskin and touched her tumbled auburn curls. Without warning his lips came down on hers in a long, bruising kiss that left her shaken and speechless. Her heart pounded as he released her, and a flood of emotion swept through her.

Words failed her and she could only gaze at him, mute with longing.

'Well, will you marry me even if I go broke?' he demanded harshly.

She found her voice.

'Philip, I'd marry you if you were a beggar,' she replied earnestly.

'Well, that's settled, then,' said Philip, clapping her briefly on the shoulders. 'Now I must go and pack. There's just one other thing, Katarina.'

'Yes?'

'Why don't you move in here while I'm gone? At least you'll have the fences to keep out reporters, and I'd like to think of you being in my home.'

'All right,' replied Kate. 'I'd like that too.'

'But don't under any circumstances let any reporters in,' warned Philip.

'I won't,' shuddered Kate. 'But don't stay away too long.'

'A week at the most,' promised Philip. 'The time will fly.'

But the time didn't fly. It dragged agonisingly. The bad weather, having once set in, seemed determined to stay. Each morning Kate woke to the noise of dripping rain, and the skies outside were grey and cloudy. Chill winds swept down from the mountains and there was no sense in venturing out with her camera. Who would want to read holiday brochures that looked as if they had been photographed in the Arctic Circle? Nor could she keep herself busy down in the hotel reception centre. Nikos, pale but determined, was back at work, typing with one hand, and Kate's Greek was still too limited to make her much use for anything else. Besides, Dorothea was determined to keep her shut up, out of reach of reporters. Small wonder that after three days Kate was thoroughly bored!

But the fourth day dawned bright and sunny and offered an unexpected diversion. One of the hotel bellboys brought the mail to the house, and Kate cheered up instantly at the sight of the four items spread out on the hall table. A colour postcard of Thessaloníki from Philip with an almost illegible scrawl that said simply 'No news is good news. Love P.' A letter from her parents, redirected from the archaeological site at Nyssa. A second letter from Tassos Astrinakis offering to buy her 'Windmills of Mykonos' photos for a greetings card series, which made her utter a cry of delight. And a package from Thessaloníki containing the prints of the photos she had taken during her holiday on the *Eleftheria*.

Carrying this booty into the sitting-room, Kate settled down to enjoy herself. The holiday snapshots brought back a flood of glorious memories, and for several minutes she was able to forget the anxiety that tormented her. Reliving those moments of sunbathing and snorkelling, of dinners in little tavernas and walks along white sandy beaches, she felt suddenly convinced that Philip would bulldoze his way through all the problems that now confronted them. And when she came to the photo of the two of them cavorting topless in the jacuzzi she laughed out loud and set it aside. Definitely one for the private photo album, as Philip had said!

But her parents' letter gave her less joy. Fortunately, in far-off Australia, they had not had the chance to read the scandalous stories about their daughter that were currently entertaining Europe, but it was obvious they were worried about her. Kate smoothed out the aerogramme and stared at her mother's small upright handwriting.

...you know we worry about you, Kate. You've been gone for over six months now, and this photography business still hasn't amounted to anything, just as we expected. Don't you think it's time you gave it up and came home? Your father's secretary Mrs Wilcox is retiring in November, and you could take over her position whenever you like. Do write and let us know...

Kate winced. Well, she would have to get it over with sooner or later. Ever since Philip's departure she had been trying to compose a letter to her parents, but every attempt had ended up in the waste-paper basket. Now she would definitely have to tackle it before her parents heard some lurid third-hand account of her relationship with Philip, on television or in a newspaper. Rummaging in a desk drawer, Kate found a writing pad and sat down on the couch. Then, chewing her pen thoughtfully, she began to write.

Dear Mum and Dad,
I know this will come as a shock to you, but I have just become engaged. My fiancé's name is Philip Andronikos and he works in the hotel industry. We met during an earthquake in the area near Mt Panagia, and had to stay overnight at a little village called Ayía Sofía because the roads were blocked by fallen stones. There was an immediate attraction between us, which has now changed to something deeper. We plan to be married in Philip's home village of Áyios Dimitrios as soon as we can arrange it with the local priest, Father Stargos. Philip and I are both hoping that you will fly over for the wedding, but please don't mention it to anybody else, as we want to keep it simple. If you——

Kate froze as there was a sudden ring at the back door of the house. She wasn't expecting any of the hotel staff at this hour of the day, and her earlier experience with the photographer had made her wary. Padding cautiously into the kitchen, she lifted the edge of the lace curtain and peered out. The man who stood grinning wryly at her was the last person she'd expected to see.

'Stavros!' she breathed, letting the curtain drop.

Her brain raced as she tried to decide what to do. Philip had categorically forbidden her to have any dealings with Stavros, but she had never really understood the reason for Philip's hostility. And, besides, it seemed so absurd to refuse to open the door when Stavros knew perfectly well that she was inside. Absurd and somehow embarrassing. As if he were the big, bad wolf and she were the little pig waiting to be eaten. But what on earth could Irene's brother possibly want with her? Might it not be just as embarrassing to speak to him?

The doorbell rang tentatively and, with an uncomfortable, fluttering feeling in her stomach, Kate made up her mind. Resolutely, she turned the handle and stood back.

'Hi, Kate, how're you doing?' asked Stavros, stepping inside with a faint swagger.

'Hello,' replied Kate warily. 'What can I do for you?'

'Hey, lighten up,' urged Stavros. 'I'm not going to eat you, honey.'

Kate coloured, feeling as if he had read her mind. 'It's just that I didn't feel you'd have much to say to me under the circumstances,' she said stiffly.

'Circumstances?' echoed Stavros blankly. 'Oh, you mean all that stuff about Irene. Yeah, well, look, in a way that's why I'm here. Is there somewhere we can talk?'

He lunged suddenly forward and, for one panic-stricken moment, Kate thought that he was about to attack her. Then she saw that he was simply helping himself to a celery stick from a bowl of cold water that stood on the counter. Weak with relief and cursing herself inwardly as a fool, she answered him disjointedly.

'Talk? Well, I don't… Perhaps you'd better come into the sitting-room.'

Once inside the sitting-room, Kate realised that she had left her unfinished letter to her parents lying on the couch. Help! The last thing she wanted was for Irene's brother to learn about her marriage plans. Hastily she closed the writing pad and thrust it away into a drawer of the sideboard. Feeling thoroughly flustered, she sank down on the couch and ushered Stavros into an armchair.

'Do sit down,' she uttered nervously.

Stavros smiled, a faint, bewildered smile, as if he was wondering what was upsetting her. Kate had just begun to settle down and breathe more calmly when a fresh source of panic attacked her. She had suddenly realised to her horror that the photo of her and Philip in the jacuzzi was still lying on the couch, half concealed by one of the cushions. If Stavros saw that there would really be an uproar. Smiling brightly, she shifted slightly along the couch until she was sitting in front of it and then let her fingers wander until they touched the photo. Still smiling, she stuffed it hastily out of sight.

'Are you OK?' asked Stavros. 'You seem kinda nervous.'

'I-I'm fine!' stammered Kate. 'Stavros, did you want to see me about anything in particular?'

Stavros shifted uncomfortably and stared down at the backs of his hands.

'Yes, I did,' he admitted. 'It's to do with Philip and Irene——'

'Well, in that case, I don't think there's anything useful to be said,' cut in Kate with spirit. 'I'm not prepared to discuss that subject with anybody!'

'Hey, wait a minute, don't get me wrong!' protested Stavros swiftly. 'Look, Kate, I don't have anything against you personally. I always liked you. I'd have to be honest and say I'm sorry that you cut out Irene where Philip's concerned, but the truth is it's really none of my business. I didn't come here to try and persuade you to drop the guy.'

'Then what did you come for?' demanded Kate suspiciously.

Stavros grinned ruefully.

'It's kind of a delicate subject,' he said. 'But it's like this: you know the necklace that Philip gave Irene on the night of the hotel opening?'

'Yes,' said Kate apprehensively. 'What about it?'

Stavros looked embarrassed.

'Well, Irene left it here at Philip's house the night of the opening. In his bedroom actually.'

Kate felt a pang of pure jealousy so searing that it almost scorched her. She knew perfectly well that Philip and Irene had been engaged for years, but somehow the thought that he might have slept with Irene even after he'd met Kate had never occurred to her. And yet they had seemed awfully close on the night of the opening . . . Biting her lip, she cast Stavros a stricken look.

'So?' she asked unsteadily.

'So Irene wants me to collect it for her,' replied Stavros. 'Hell, I'm sorry, Kate. I know it's kind of embarrassing for you, but it's not too great for me either. And Irene could hardly come and get it herself, could she?'

'I suppose not,' agreed Kate bitterly.

'So, is it OK if I go up and get it?' persisted Stavros.

Kate hesitated. She wanted to shout that Irene could drop dead before she would get the necklace, but she had too much dignity to make such a fool of herself. Besides, some innate sense of fairness made it impossible for her to keep someone else's property out of spite.

'I suppose so,' she said reluctantly.

All the way up the stairs she kept hoping absurdly that Stavros was wrong, that there would be no sign of the necklace in Philip's room. But the hope was vain. As they reached the top of the stairs Stavros hurried on ahead, and by the time Kate caught him up he was already standing at the dressing-table with an enamelled jewellery box open in front of him. He held up the magnificent river of diamonds that sparkled in the light.

'This is it,' he said, unceremoniously stuffing it into the sports bag that was slung over his shoulder. 'Thanks, Kate. I—— Did you hear that?'

'Hear what?' asked Kate, baffled.

'It sounded like a window opening downstairs.'

'Oh, no,' groaned Kate. 'Not more of those stupid reporters!'

She hurried downstairs and ran from room to room, checking all the windows, but there was no sign of an intruder. But perhaps she had just frightened him off and he was still lurking outside, waiting for his chance... Looking anxiously round the dining-room, she heard a footstep behind her and jumped.

'Oh, Stavros!' she exclaimed. 'You gave me such a fright!'

'Kate, you're all on edge,' he said sympathetically. 'You shouldn't let those reporters get under your skin so much. They always write a load of garbage about rich people, but nobody believes it. Look, why don't you come down and have a game of tennis with me? It'll take your mind off all this.'

Kate hesitated.

'Come on,' urged Stavros, smiling disarmingly. 'I promise I'll personally check all the locks and bolts for you before we go.'

'All right,' agreed Kate, her spirits rising. 'Why not?'

The next hour was spent furiously pounding a ball backwards and forwards across the net. The hard surface of the courts had dried quickly after the rain, and Kate found the exercise invigorating. Out in the sunlight her earlier fears about reporters seemed ridiculous, and even her worries about Philip's financial problems receded. When a hotel employee came out to tell Stavros there was a telephone call for him, Kate felt quite surprised to find that it was after one o'clock.

'Do you want to call it quits now?' asked Stavros, smiling at her with perfect white teeth. 'Or should we go on playing later?'

'Well, it is lunchtime,' said Kate regretfully.

'And I'm winning,' agreed Stavros. 'Which is always a good reason to stop playing.'

Just for an instant there was something almost wolf-like about his smile. Kate's marrow seemed to freeze in her bones as she looked into those glittering dark eyes, then Stavros deliberately stretched, blinked, and smiled at her again so cheekily that she felt a complete fool.

'Are you sure you wouldn't like me to come back up to the house with you and check for bogymen under the beds?' he teased.

'No, I can handle it,' she answered pertly. '*Yasu*, Stavros.'

'*Ya.*'

On her way back to the house she wondered idly why Philip seemed so hostile towards Stavros. No doubt he was a bit of a playboy, but he had tremendous warmth and charm. Did Philip resent that? Or was he jealous of the way Stavros's life had always been so easy and cushioned compared to his own? Anyway, whatever the reason, it was totally absurd and archaic for Philip to forbid her to see Stavros.

Kate was still musing on this when she reached the front door of the house. A quick glance at the shrubbery reassured her that there were no reporters lurking in the bushes and, with a sigh of relief, she inserted her key into the massive front door. But before she even had time to turn the key, the door opened slowly in front of her. Kate gave a little cry of alarm and stepped backwards at the sight of the figure that confronted her.

'You!' she breathed in dismay. 'What are you doing here?'

It was her ex-lover, Leon Clark. He was a tall, good-looking man with long brown hair, which flopped forward over his forehead and eyes of a deep corn-flower-blue. And he was smiling charmingly. But the smile held as much appeal for Kate as a crocodile's.

'*Yasu!*' he said mockingly. 'Aren't you going to give me a kiss, sweetheart? After all, it's a long time since you've seen dear old Leon, isn't it?'

'Not long enough!' retorted Kate angrily. 'Where did you spring from, you creep?'

He brandished a nail-file teasingly.

'Well, let's just say I found a window that wasn't quite secure,' he smirked.

'So you've added breaking and entering to your talents of lying and adultery, have you?' demanded Kate disdainfully. 'Well, I don't know what good you think it will do you, Leon. All I have to do is call hotel security and they'll throw you out so fast that it will make your head spin!'

'That would be a pity,' murmured Leon. 'Particularly since I haven't had a chance to put my business proposition to you.'

'I know all about your propositions, Leon,' said Kate coolly. 'And I'm not interested in them, business or otherwise.'

'Not even in a hundred thousand dollars for the exclusive rights to your story? This love-affair with Andronikos is big news, you know, Kate.'

'A hundred thousand dollars!' echoed Kate in disgust. 'Don't be ridiculous, Leon! Reputable television stations don't have that kind of money, and they don't deal in slander.'

'I'm not with that sort of television station any longer. I'm with the commercial media. Stardust International, based in London. And they're offering a hundred thousand dollars for the exclusive rights to your story. More, if you'll supply pictures.'

'If they were offering a hundred million dollars I still wouldn't be interested, Leon. My story, as you keep calling it, is not for sale.'

'Oh, but mine is, sweetheart,' said Leon softly, moving a step closer to her and catching her by the wrist. 'It's not quite as juicy as yours, but I'll bet there are a lot of readers who'd pay good money to hear all about our cosy little love-nest in Paddington, Sydney, before you really hit the big time.'

'You swine!' hissed Kate. 'You wouldn't dare!'

'Wouldn't I?' demanded Leon coldly. 'Just watch me, darling. I've been waiting for a break like this for years. And nothing's going to stop me cashing in on it. Unless your new boyfriend would rather pay me not to tell my story.'

'Get out!' cried Kate.

With a strength she didn't know she possessed, she ran at him and swatted him hard with her tennis racquet. Then, wrestling him off balance, she leapt across the threshold, pushed him out of the door and slammed it shut behind him. Feverishly she shot the bolts and then ran to the back door of the house and did the same. Only when she had checked every window in the house did she collapse, shaking, in a chair. And even then she had to leap up a moment later.

'Oh, help, the jacuzzi photo... my letter!' she cried, panic-stricken.

But this time her luck was in. For when she raced frantically into the sitting-room and scrabbled under the sofa cushion the photo was undisturbed. And a quick check of the sideboard drawer showed that her letter to her parents was also safe. Weak with relief, she sank down on the scattered cushions, clutching the photo. Her heart was pounding as if she had run a marathon, and an awful sense of impending disaster hung over her.

'Oh, I wish Philip would come back!' she groaned.

But it was another two days before Philip came back, and one look at his face told Kate that his errand had not prospered. His lips were set in a thin line and his eyes wore an intent, brooding look. Dropping his overnight bag on the hall floor, he took Kate in his arms and kissed her fiercely. His unshaven jaw rasped her sensitive skin and she winced involuntarily.

'Sorry,' said Philip roughly. 'I didn't have time to shave this morning. There were bankers to meet. And after that I wanted to see you so badly that I just climbed in the car and drove like a madman. I'll go up now and get to work with a razor.'

'Wait!' cried Kate, clutching his jacket. 'Philip, it doesn't matter. I just want to hold you, to be with you. You look so exhausted. Didn't... didn't it go well?'

He gave a harsh laugh and ran his fingers through his springy dark hair.

'They're a lot of fools, Katarina!' he exclaimed. 'They can't see a golden opportunity when it's right in front of them. Not one of them!'

'So there's no hope, then?' faltered Kate.

'Don't say that!' snapped Philip. 'I can't stand that sort of defeatist talk. I'm not beaten yet by a long shot. I've still got one more idea that I'm going to try.'

Kate nodded, only half listening. However urgent Philip's financial problems, there was something else that worried her even more. For the last two days she had been fretting about her unexpected encounters with Stavros and Leon. Try as she might, she could not rid herself of a sharp sense of jealousy about Irene and the necklace, while Leon Clark's visit had plunged her into even worse confusion. After two sleepless nights she was still unable to make up her mind whether to tell Philip everything or simply say nothing about the incidents. Philip was hardly likely to be pleased that she had had a visit from an ex-lover, but perhaps it was better to be honest with him. Taking a deep breath, she steeled herself for the ordeal of confiding in him.

'Philip, there's something I ought to tell you——' she began.

'Can it wait till we've eaten?' cut in Philip. 'I haven't had a meal since last night, and I'm pretty tired from travelling. Why don't you call one of the chefs and order dinner while I take a shower? Then we can talk.'

'Yes, of course,' agreed Kate remorsefully. 'I cooked some stiphado today myself, if you'd like to try that. Or I can phone one of the hotel restaurants if you'd rather have something else.'

Her voice was hesitant, but she looked up at him eagerly. A warm smile lit his face.

'Oh, Kate,' he said softly. 'How did you get so sweet and anxious to please me? Of course I'll try the stiphado.'

When he came downstairs half an hour later the house was filled with the rich aroma of stewed beef, tomatoes, herbs and crusty bread. Kate found the formal dining-room overpowering, so she had set a small, cosy table in the breakfast nook. Philip nodded appreciatively as he sat down.

'This reminds me of my mother's cottage,' he said, gazing down at the traditional Greek tablecloth. 'In fact it even smells like my mother's cottage.'

Kate set out a large dish of potatoes baked with lemon and rosemary, and a hearty salad of black olives, tomatoes, cucumbers and feta cheese to accompany the stew, and then sat down opposite him.

'*Kali oreksi,*' she murmured, picking up her fork.

They ate in companionable silence and Philip demolished three large helpings of food before he finally pushed away his plate with a contented sigh.

'Bravo,' he said. 'That was excellent.'

Kate gave a troubled smile.

'Thanks,' she said absent-mindedly.

'But something is troubling you, isn't it?' demanded Philip shrewdly. 'This thing that you want to discuss with me?'

Kate nodded unhappily.

'Is it to do with Stavros?' asked Philip sharply, seizing a bread roll and tearing off a large hunk.

Kate gave him a startled glance.

'How did you know?' she demanded.

Philip frowned angrily.

'You surely didn't think you could play tennis with him for a full hour in front of the reception centre and not have anybody notice, did you?' he demanded. 'I've told you before, Kate, and I'll tell you again—I won't have you associating with that young man. Under no circumstances are you to be alone with him, is that clear?'

Philip's expression was so fierce that Kate quailed. What on earth would he say if he knew Stavros had been alone in the house with her? Perhaps it would be better if she waited for some other time to discuss it.

'All right, Philip,' she said in a subdued voice. 'Shall I make some coffee now?'

Philip's anger seemed to evaporate instantly.

'Please,' he agreed. 'And take no notice of me if I snap, Katarina. I'm tired and worried.'

Kate switched on some soft Greek Remvetika music and they sat drinking coffee until at last their cups were empty. Philip gave a sigh of satisfaction.

'That was a superb meal,' he said bluntly. 'You will make a good wife, Katarina.'

'Provided I remember my place and stay in the kitchen?' demanded Kate challengingly.

Philip gave her a sidelong glance full of lust.

'I might also allow you to warm my bed,' he murmured throatily.

Reaching out one powerful arm, he caught her by the wrist and drew her towards him. The movement made his dressing-gown fall open, exposing his dark, hairy chest and gold neck-chain. Kate's heart began to pound wildly, and trickles of excitement ran down her spine.

'I don't believe you're wearing anything under that dressing-gown,' she murmured.

'Why don't you come and see?' demanded Philip.

Pulling her down on to his lap, he caught her face between his hands and kissed her violently. She heard his low groan of excitement as her lips parted against his, then he was wrestling with her dress, forcing open the bodice and slipping his hands inside. A thrill of desire went through her as he touched her naked breasts. His fingers moved over her nipples, teasing them into hard, tingling peaks, then he bent his head and went to work with his tongue. Only when she was gasping and whimpering with longing did he finally take pity on her.

'I think it's time you came and warmed my bed,' he growled huskily.

Taking her by the hand, he led her upstairs to the bedroom. Lifting her bodily off her feet, he flung her down on the bed, stripped her clothes off her and flung them aside. Then he stood gazing down at her with narrowed dark eyes. His breath was coming hard and fast as if he had run in a long and gruelling race, and there was no longer any sign of humour in his face.

'I'm going to make you mine, body and soul, Katarina,' he said fiercely. 'And if you ever do this with another man I swear I will kill him.'

His intensity frightened her and she shrank back against the pillows, smiling uncertainly.

'Don't joke like that, Philip,' she pleaded.

'It's no joke,' he replied grimly.

Then with a single swift movement he tore off his dressing-gown and climbed on to the bed beside her. Hesitantly she reached out her arms to him, but she found herself swept into an embrace that both thrilled and alarmed her. It was useless for Philip to pretend that he was tame and civilised like the men she had known in the past. Her own body, melting and throbbing and crying out under his caresses, told her differently. He was a man as primitive and passionate as the land which had borne him. And, as he brought her to a moaning, sobbing climax more intense than any she had ever experienced, Kate knew that she would not want it any other way.

Coming slowly down to earth and finding her fingers tangled in his thick, dark hair, Kate smiled through her tears. His body was hard and lean and powerful on top of her, his heart was pounding wildly against her, and her name still lingered on his lips. Soon, very soon, they would be man and wife. A profound sense of joy and contentment welled up inside her.

'I'm so glad you're back, Philip,' she whispered fervently. 'Now I'm sure that nothing can go wrong.'

CHAPTER EIGHT

THEY were lingering over breakfast on the terrace the following morning when the bombshell struck. It was a perfect morning. Sunlight danced on the blue waters of the sea, birds sang in the trees, scarlet geraniums rioted over the edges of their terracotta urns. And the air was filled with the mingled fragrance of hot coffee, sesame rolls, and sweet honeysuckle. Yet the moment Kate heard the garden gate clang shut and saw Dorothea hurrying up the path she knew instinctively that something had gone horribly wrong.

'I've never seen Dorothea look so agitated,' she said anxiously, crossing to the edge of the terrace. 'I wonder what's happened.'

'Probably nothing serious,' replied Philip.

But he too rose to his feet and moved across to meet Dorothea as she came panting up the steps, brandishing a newspaper.

'What is it?' he demanded. 'More of Irene's antics?'

'Worse!' replied Dorothea, thrusting it into his hands and turning a hostile glance on Kate. 'How could you?' she said with a catch in her voice. Then, pressing a handkerchief to her face, she fled towards the hotel.

Baffled, Kate turned back to Philip. To her dismay she saw his initial calm give way to violent outrage as his eyes skimmed down the page. He swore softly in Greek, and his powerful hands crumpled the newspaper into a shapeless mass.

'What is it?' asked Kate, appalled. 'What does it say?'

His head came up, and the rage in his eyes terrified her.

'Do you really need to ask?' he demanded brutally. 'Surely Stardust's hottest reporter Leon Clark told you what he was going to write when you sold him the interview?'

'Leon?' echoed Kate in horror. 'Oh, no, I don't believe it!'

Her legs seemed to buckle beneath her. She collapsed dizzily into a chair, feeling as sick and faint as if somebody had punched her in the stomach.

'What does it say?' she whispered again.

'Read it!' retorted Philip savagely.

He thrust the mangled newspaper in front of her and strode across to the balustrade, where he stood with his palms outspread and his jaw clenched. Kate cast one swift, agonised glance at his angry profile and then smoothed out the crumpled paper and began to read. Almost at once she had to stop, as a violent trembling overtook her.

'I can't!' she breathed, clapping her hands over her mouth.

'Too sensitive to read it, are you?' snarled Philip. 'Well, let me oblige!'

He tore the newspaper out of her unresisting hands and paced around the terrace, his voice resonant with fury as he read out the offending headlines.

'AUSTRALIAN SEX KITTEN TO WED GREECE'S MOST ELIGIBLE BACHELOR?

Stardust International's hottest reporter Leon Clark offered unknown photographer Kate Walsh $100,000 for the exclusive rights to her life story. Walsh, a Sydneysider, hit the headlines when she ousted Greek heiress Irene Marmara in the affections of Greek multi-millionaire Philip Andronikos. According to Walsh, the romance is serious. She and Andronikos plan to tie the knot in the village church at Áyios Dimitrios before Christmas. To learn all about the girl from Down Under who ousted an heiress, turn to page fifteen for Kate Walsh's life story, illustrated by her own frank and fearless photos...'

Philip paused and looked down at Kate with a glance that froze her to the marrow.

'You disgust me!' he said contemptuously. 'Do you mean to tell me you even sold them photos?'

'I didn't sell them anything!' blazed Kate. 'You can't possibly believe this lunacy, Philip!'

But Philip was already leafing furiously through the newspaper and did not deign to answer her. Then suddenly his search came to an abrupt end. With a low gasp of anger he looked across at her, and his gaze seemed to cut through her like a knife.

'Oh, no?' he said softly. 'Then how do you explain this, Katarina?'

His forefinger stabbed the page, but for a moment Kate's eyes were so blurred by tears that she could see nothing. Then she blinked and the full horror of Leon's treachery became clear to her. There, in the middle of the newspaper for everyone to see, was the joyful portrait of her and Philip in the jacuzzi. She gave a gasp of dismay.

'I don't understand this!' she exclaimed in bewilderment. 'Leon wasn't even in the sitting-room. Only in the front hall.'

'So he did come here, did he?' demanded Philip. 'And you gave him all this information?'

'Yes,' said Kate in a dazed voice. 'I mean...no. He was here, Philip, but only at the front door. I told him to go away. Of course I didn't give him anything.'

'Then how do you explain this photo?' insisted Philip.

'I can't explain it!' cried Kate wildly. 'I don't understand it myself. I stuffed the photo down the sofa cushions and I didn't think he'd seen it, because it was still there later. But he must have taken a photo of it.'

Philip shook his head at this tangled explanation.

'Why did you stuff it down the sofa?' he asked.

'Because somebody came to the front door and I didn't want him to see it.'

'Leon Clark?' demanded Philip.

'No. Somebody else.'

She flushed, conscious that any mention of Stavros could only worsen her case.

'Who?' demanded Philip relentlessly.

'Stavros!' she blurted out.

Seeing Philip's face harden, she babbled on. 'Stavros came to ask me to play tennis and I went down to the courts with him.'

'That was all?' rapped out Philip. 'He didn't come inside?'

Kate hesitated. The thought of the necklace disturbed her, but she pushed it away. She was in enough trouble with Philip already.

'No!' she said sharply.

'Go on,' ordered Philip. 'How does this Clark fellow come into all this? Who is he? What connection does he have with you? Or is he a total stranger?'

Kate let out a long, ragged sigh.

'He was a current-affairs reporter,' she said wearily. 'He came out from Britain last year to join a TV station in Sydney. I was one of the camera crew for his programme and we were thrown together a good deal at work. We started going out together and eventually one thing led to another. Our affair lasted three or four months, and then one night he invited me out to dinner. He said he had something special he wanted to say to me.' Her voice wobbled.

'Go on,' insisted Philip in a hard voice.

'I thought he was going to ask me to marry him. Silly, isn't it? Instead he told me, oh, so casually, that his wife and children would be coming out to Australia to join him within a month, but that we could still keep our affair going provided we were discreet about it.'

'What did you do?' asked Philip.

Kate tossed her head.

'Oh, I behaved very discreetly!' she said through clenched teeth. 'I told him to drop dead, dumped a plateful of hot moussaka into his lap and stormed out of the restaurant. Two days later I received my retrenchment notice.'

'You think he was behind it?' demanded Philip.

Kate shrugged.

'Probably,' she said wearily. 'Anyway, that was the last I saw of him until he showed up here. I didn't even realise he'd left Australia.'

She cast a swift, apprehenisve glance at Philip. Ever since their dinner together at Porto Carras she had agonised over whether she should tell him about Leon. And deep down she had expected some kind of stormy response from him if he ever heard the news. Rage, jealousy, even sympathy, perhaps. Instead he was treating her to a cold, impassive scrutiny and the only sign of emotion on his face was the tightening of the muscles around his mouth.

'So how did this...ex-lover of yours get into my house?' he rapped out.

Kate took a deep breath.

'I don't really know,' she admitted. 'I went out for a while, and when I came back he was already here. He told me he'd forced one of the windows with a nail-file.'

Philip gave a sharp bark of laughter.

'A nail-file!' he said scornfully. 'You'll have to think of a better story than that, Kate! Those are security windows. Nobody could possibly break in through them with a nail-file.'

Kate's lips trembled.

'Well, maybe I hadn't locked one of them properly!' she cried. 'How do I know? All I know is that I found Leon Clark here in the entrance hall, he made me his slimy proposition about exclusive rights for my story and I told him to get lost. I thought it was all over and done with. Instead I wake up and find all this awful stuff in the paper about me, not to mention that horrible photo. And now you seem to think I wanted all this to happen. I just can't bear it, Philip!'

Her voice rose as she came to an end, and she choked on a sudden rending sob. Burying her face in her hands, she wept despairingly. There was a long silence, broken only by her soft, gulping breaths. Then Philip's hand came slowly down on her shoulder.

'So you didn't ever invite Leon Clark inside or deliberately tell him any of this?' he demanded sternly.

She raised her tear-stained face to his and shook her head.

'Of course I didn't!' she said vehemently. 'You must believe me, Philip!'

There was another long silence, then Philip gave a long, shuddering sigh.

'Whatever I may or may not believe,' he said at last, 'I'm going to crucify Leon Clark for writing this stuff about us. Give me that paper. My lawyers will need it.'

Swallowing, Kate picked up the newspaper and turned to pass it to him. But Philip had maltreated it so badly that it was falling to pieces, and as it changed hands a single sheet fluttered free. Philip bent to retrieve it. As he straightened up his face turned ashen with fury.

'I thought you said you only saw Clark at the door?' he murmured dangerously.

'Y-yes,' agreed Kate, mystified.

'Then how the hell do you explain this?' snarled Philip.

He held the single page in front of her, and she gave a cry of disbelief. In the centre of it was a photo of herself in a lacy nightdress, lying seductively on her side in the middle of Philip's huge four-poster bed. Perched on the bed beside her, with one hand on her naked shoulder, was Leon Clark. Above the photo was the caption 'Kate Walsh shows her paces for Stardust reporter Leon Clark.'

Kate gave a groan of dismay.

'That unprincipled swine!' she cried. 'It's a trick photo, Philip. He took it in Sydney last year, and he's obviously superimposed it on a shot of your bedroom... It's quite an easy technique—any photographer could do it.'

But Philip was staring at her bleakly.

'Y-you don't believe me, do you?' she faltered.

He gave a hoarse groan, somewhere between a laugh and a cry of pain.

'No, I don't!' he said savagely. 'And to think you almost fooled me! The tears, the white face, the quivering lips... You missed your vocation, Kate. You should have been an actress, not a photographer. But this is too much even for me to swallow.'

He turned scornfully away and strode towards the house.

'Philip!' she cried desperately, springing after him.

He paused, with her hand on his sleeve.

'It just won't wash, Kate,' he said sadly, looking down at her with liquid dark eyes. 'Rather a pity, really. Do you know, I really thought you were different from other women? That you really cared about me? But you're just as bad as the rest of them—only interested in money and fame and notoriety. Why did you decide to sell out on me, Kate? Was it because you thought I was going broke? I could have made another fortune, you know. You didn't have to betray me like this for a miserable hundred thousand.'

'It's not true, Philip,' whispered Kate in an agonised voice. 'I didn't betray you. I'd never do such a thing!'

'Wouldn't you?' said Philip contemptuously. 'I'm sorry, *agapimou*, but I just don't trust those big green eyes and those little quivering lips any more. So why don't you just take yourself off and we'll call it quits?'

Kate stared at him, aghast, but pride was beginning to stir inside her.

'All right,' she said through her teeth. 'If that's what you want, that's fine with me!'

'Good!' replied Philip cuttingly. 'I'll tell Dorothea to make up your cheque for the photographs and you can collect it from the office.'

'Don't bother!' retorted Kate. 'I wouldn't take money from you if I had to starve first!'

And, turning on her heel, she rushed inside to pack.

By the time Kate climbed aboard the bus from Áyios Dimitrios a curious aching numbness had replaced her earlier rage and despair. She was conscious of a couple of furtive glances from the handful of curious villagers on board, but she turned her head away and took no notice. Yet, as the bus climbed up the winding road leading from the Hotel Ariadne to the highway, she felt a brief pang of misery so intense that she bit her lip and clenched her fists until her nails dug into her skin. Leaning her head against the cool glass of the window, she gazed back at the place that had come to mean so much to her. A brief whiff of pine needles assailed her, she caught a glimpse of a sapphire-blue swimming-pool, then it all vanished behind her.

The next two hours passed in a daze for Kate. There was only one possible place she could go. Too proud to accept payment from Philip, she had hardly any money, but she knew she would find refuge at the archaeological dig. She remembered Charlie's warm invitation at their parting: 'Now remember, you can always come back here if things don't work out at Áyios Dimitrios... you're always welcome.' The trouble was that she felt so raw and humiliated that she didn't even want to face her friends. As the bus jolted over the rough country roads she came to a painful decision. Her airline ticket back to Australia was still in the money belt around her neck. True, she wasn't due to fly back until just before Christmas. But she would change her booking and go straight home.

The wild, beautiful Greek countryside flashed past her, unseen. She scarcely noticed the sunlight striking the sea and turning it to shades of gold and lavender, the purple heather, the white villages, the brown floppy-eared goats scattering out of the path of the bus. All she could see was a dark, angry face and brown eyes that blazed with scorn. She had left Philip Andronikos readily enough, but it was not so easy to leave her memories behind.

At last the bus came to a halt in the village square at Nyssa. The recent rain had left huge muddy ruts in the dirt road, and the driver had to back the bus carefully round a corner to avoid bogging it. As Kate climbed down she recognised one of the workmen from the archaeological site, dressed in his best clothes and chatting to a friend under a fig tree.

'*Yasu*, Angelos,' she said. 'Where is Dr Lucas? *Pou ine Kyria Lucas? Ine etho?*'

He looked baffled.

'*Ohi. Dhen ine edho. Ine i Kiriaki simera.*'

Kate groaned.

'She's not here because it's Sunday today?' she asked. 'What about Andrew? Kyrios Cameron?'

'*Ne,*' replied Angelos. '*Kyrios Cameron ine edho.*'

'You mean Andrew is still here?' cried Kate. 'Oh, thank goodness!'

Leaving her backpack at the café near the village square, she hitched her camera bag over her shoulder and began the long climb up through the village to the archaeologists' rented house. She had been dreading the stares of the villagers, but she need not have worried. People evidently did not read newspapers in Nyssa, or at any rate not the sort of newspapers that Leon Clark produced. Everywhere she went she was greeted by courteous smiles and cries of '*Kalimera!*' Children ran out of houses, shouting, 'Hello! What your name?' and danced along beside her. Even a stray dog with a matted black coat and a deep bark bounded up to escort her.

She could not help feeling slightly cheered by the welcome.

When she reached the house Andrew was standing at the mesh table on the terrace, sorting fragments of pottery. Catching sight of her, he dropped a large terracotta handle and came hurrying over to meet her.

'Oh, Kate!' he cried, folding her in a bony hug. 'That swine Clark ought to be hung, drawn and quartered! I tried to telephone you this morning, but I couldn't get through.'

'You've seen the papers, then?' asked Kate shakily.

He nodded glumly.

'Cheer up, love,' he said with false heartiness. 'The bubbles in the jacuzzi hid just about everything, and nobody takes any notice of that yellow Press rubbish anyway.'

'Philip did,' said Kate with a catch in her voice.

'Oh, no!' exclaimed Andrew. 'How could he be such a fool? Look, Katey, you're just about all in. Sit down and I'll make you a cup of tea and you can tell me everything. The others have gone to Kavala for a few days, so at least you'll get a bit of peace here.'

It was comforting to sit at the marble-topped table sipping lemon tea, while Andrew listened and nodded and murmured sympathetically. Bit by bit it all came out. Kate knew she could trust Andrew, and she held nothing back. Stavros, Leon, the violent quarrel with Philip—she told him everything.

'So what do you think you'll do now?' he asked when at last she came to a halt.

She shrugged and bit her lip.

'Go back to Australia, I suppose,' she said with a sigh. 'What else can I do?'

'Come off it, Kate!' said Andrew impatiently. 'It's not like you to give in so easily. You've always been a fighter.'

'What is there to fight for now?' retorted Kate. 'It's all finished, Andrew!'

'Do you still love this guy?' asked Andrew thoughtfully.

'He's the most arrogant, insensitive, self-opinionated swine I've ever met!' replied Kate hotly. 'If he crawled over broken glass for two miles to apologise to me I still wouldn't listen to him!'

Andrew grinned wryly.

'So you do,' he said. 'Just as I thought! All right, Katey, there's only one thing to be done. As soon as siesta-time finishes, you and I are going down to the OTE office and we're going to telephone Philip Andronikos.'

'What?' demanded Kate. 'Are you out of your mind, Andrew?'

Andrew cowered comically with his hands protectively over his head.

'Look,' he said reasonably, 'if Andronikos is half as aggressive and pig-headed as you are, Kate, he's not going to make the first move, is he? But I'll bet my bottom dollar that he's just kicking himself by now for driving you away. He's probably dying for a chance to make up the quarrel.'

Kate hesitated.

'Do you really think so?' she asked shyly.

'Absolutely,' agreed Andrew firmly. 'So will you let me phone him?'

A smile spread slowly over her face.

'Anything to keep you happy, Andrew,' she said.

The afternoon dragged interminably. Desperate for something to do, Kate painted collection tins, scrubbed potsherds and drew spindle whorls until her eyes watered, but her mind was not on her tasks. At last Andrew announced that it was five o'clock, and she shot out of her chair and picked up her camera bag. Although she did not say so, she was secretly hoping that she would soon be on her way back to Áyios Dimitrios.

'Ready?' asked Andrew.

'Ready!' she agreed with a radiant smile.

'Maybe you'd better let me put the call through first,' warned Andrew as they entered the telephone company office. 'If we have any trouble getting through the Hotel Ariadne switchboard my Greek is better than yours. Besides, I might be able to soften Andronikos up a bit for you.'

'OK,' agreed Kate.

Her stomach was churning with nerves as she took her place in the plastic phone booth next to Andrew. The door wouldn't close properly with two of them in the booth, and there were four or five other people in the office chatting to the OTE man or waiting for incoming calls, so that Kate couldn't help wishing for more privacy. But she comforted herself with the thought that her conversation with Philip would be in English, so nobody was likely to understand much of it.

'Parakalo?' said Andrew. 'Is that the Hotel Ariadne switchboard? May I speak to Philip Andronikos, please? No, I'm not a reporter. I'm a friend of Katherine Walsh. Tell him my name is Andrew Cameron.'

There was a long pause, then Andrew gave Kate an encouraging thumbs-up.

'Mr Andronikos? I don't know if you remember me. My name is Andrew Cameron and we met briefly when you came to Nyssa to see Kate. Look, I know this is none of my business, but I'm really upset to see Kate in this condition. She's absolutely devastated by this quarrel she's had with you and I don't blame her. I've known Kate for twenty years and, let me tell you, there's no possible way she could have done the things you're accusing her of. I've tried to talk sense to her, but she says she's going back to Australia as soon as she can get a flight out. The thing is I'm sure she still loves you. Will you at least talk to her about it?'

There was another long pause and then Andrew handed over the receiver. Kate's insides clenched with nerves and her voice shook as she spoke.

'Hello, Philip?'

'Hello, Kate.'

His voice was no longer angry, but it wasn't friendly either. It was cool, wary, restrained, as if he were discussing a business deal.

'I hear you're thinking of going back to Australia?' he said.

'Yes.' Her own voice was so low and husky that she could hardly hear it herself.

'What about your photography?'

'I think I'll chuck it in. My father's offered me a job as a secretary. I was never much good at it anyway.'

'That's not true! You were damned good!'

That was more like the Philip Andronikos she knew. Arrogant, emphatic, overbearing. A strangled sound escaped her, half-laughter, half-sob.

'What did you say?' he demanded instantly.

'Nothing.'

'You didn't pick up your cheque from the office.'

'I told you before—I won't take money from you!' she retorted fiercely.

'Don't be so damned stupid! You earned that money. The photos you took for the brochures were very good. Anyway, what are you going to live on if you don't accept it?'

'I'm all right,' she said defensively. 'I'm with friends and I'll pay them back if I have to borrow anything. They know they can trust me.'

There was another long pause. Then Philip's voice came down the line, harsh, almost resentful.

'Perhaps I was a bit too hasty this morning, Katarina. But you did tell me some pretty unbelievable things.'

Kate could hear the suspicion, the uncertainty, as clearly as if she were with him. This wasn't the apology she wanted! More like a re-run of the accusations.

'Does that mean you're telling me you're sorry?' she demanded.

'No!' snarled Philip. 'Damn it, Kate! You're the one who should be apologising, not me! But I think we ought to get together and talk some time soon.'

Kate's heart somersaulted wildly.

'Now?' she asked. 'Will you come to Nyssa?'

'I can't, Kate. I've got a business meeting in half an hour's time about the hotel finances. But I could send Yannis with the car to bring you over tomorrow.'

'No, Philip,' said Kate slowly. 'I'm not setting foot in Áyios Dimitrios again until I know that things are already sorted out between us. It would simply be too painful and humiliating. I'm not going back there until I know that you trust me absolutely.'

'How can I, Kate?' demanded Philip. 'How can I trust you after what you've just done to me?'

'You still believe all that rubbish, don't you?' cried Kate wildly. 'All right, Philip, that's it! It's a total waste of time for us to try and get back together. I just can't live with that sort of suspicion festering between us. Maybe one of these days you'll find out that I didn't sell you out to the media, but I won't be here to see it. I'm going back to Australia! *Addio*!'

With a thunderous crash she slammed down the phone and burst into tears. Andrew and the OTE man flinched and exchanged sympathetic glances.

'Oh, Kate!' said Andrew wearily. 'What on earth did you do that for? He was just starting to come round. Well, it's no use crying. Come on, let's go and think about what we're going to do next.'

He paid the OTE man and shepherded the weeping Kate out of the door.

'I hate him!' she cried savagely as they found themselves in the muddy square outside.

'I know,' said Andrew soothingly. 'But it'll all come right, you'll see.'

'It won't,' wailed Kate.

Andrew looked around him with a harassed expression.

'Shall we go back home and have some more tea?'

'I don't want any tea!' raged Kate.

'Well, what do you want?' asked Andrew.

'I want to go home!' she cried. 'Back to Australia where nobody has even heard any of this awful stuff they're writing about me. Where I'll never have to see Philip Andronikos in my life again!'

Andrew stared at her, aghast.

'Are you sure?' he demanded. 'What about your photography?'

Kate leaned her head against the peeling, whitewashed wall of the OTE office and gave a deep, hopeless sigh.

'I just don't care any more, Andy,' she said huskily. 'And that's the truth.'

Then she fished inside the open neck of her shirt and pulled out a money belt. Opening the zip pocket, she drew out an airline ticket. Tears filled her eyes.

'Could you do me one more favour?' she asked. 'I've got an open return ticket to Sydney with Qantas. Could you phone their office and book me on the next possible flight out of Athens?'

Andrew winced.

'Whatever you say,' he agreed reluctantly.

It was not quite seven o'clock when Kate and Andrew made their way into the village square the following morning. Andrew cast a worried glance at his companion. She was deathly pale, and ever since the telephone call the day before she had been acting like a sleepwalker. She had thanked him listlessly for handling her travel arrangements and had agreed to everything he'd suggested. Yes, it was a good idea to leave her pack overnight at the café next to the bus-stop instead of lugging it back to the house for the night. No, she didn't want him to make another call to Philip. Yes, she would write as soon as she reached Sydney. Sensing her despair, Andrew could do nothing but give her a clumsy squeeze on the arm and pray for the bus to arrive.

When it finally lurched up the rutted road and came to a halt under the large fig tree at the edge of the square, Kate showed her first sign of animation in hours. Flinging her arms around Andrew, she gave him a fierce hug.

'Thanks for everything, Andy!' she said urgently. 'It's good to know that there's somebody who doesn't believe the worst of me. Look, if you ever see Philip Andronikos again, tell him...tell him... No, never mind!'

Her voice broke off on a sob. Swallowing hard, she darted across the square towards the café.

'I must get my pack!' she said in a muffled voice. 'The bus will be leaving in a couple of minutes.'

Her backpack was still on the front terrace of the café, where she had left it the previous day. Bending down, Kate seized it by one of the shoulder straps. But as she did so a hand closed around her wrist. Startled, she looked up and saw the local policeman gazing suspiciously down at her. He said something to her in Greek, which she did not understand.

'What did he say, Andrew?'

'He wants to know if you're the owner of this pack.'

Kate's face cleared. She smiled. 'Yes, I am,' she said distinctly. 'I'm not stealing it. *Ine thikimou*. It's mine!'

But the policeman was speaking again, saying something she could not grasp. And Andrew's face was changing to a mask of frozen horror.

'No!' cried Andrew. 'No! That's ridiculous.'

'What is it?' demanded Kate, her voice sharp with alarm. 'What did he say, Andrew?'

There was a moment's silence, then Andrew's reply came back full of disbelief.

'He said he's placing you under arrest for the possession of heroin.'

CHAPTER NINE

'HEROIN?' echoed Kate in horror. 'But that's ridiculous... I've never in my life... What on earth does he mean?'

The policeman was speaking rapidly now, delving into her backpack and holding up a tin of talcum powder. Andrew's mouth hung slack as he tried to follow the fluent Greek from Kate's accuser.

'He says that last night he had an anonymous telephone tip-off that the owner of this backpack was smuggling heroin hidden inside a talcum-powder tin. He says he'll have to hold you in custody until the contents of the tin have been analysed in Thessaloníki.'

'But that's ridiculous!' protested Kate. 'Anyway, that talcum powder isn't even mine. I never use the stuff... I'm allergic to most of it.'

She looked down at the red and black tin, blazoned with the brand name Fresco. She knew she had seen it somewhere before... Of course! It was the complimentary brand supplied at the Hotel Ariadne.

'Somebody must have set me up, Andrew!' she cried, her voice sharp with panic. 'Somebody from the Hotel Ariadne. Tell him, explain to him!'

But it was obvious that the policeman was not going to be easily convinced. He simply shrugged his shoulders, filled in a label, which he stuck to the talcum-powder tin before placing it in a bag, and then produced a pair of handcuffs.

'No!' cried Kate.

She whirled around, ready for a panic-stricken attempt to flee. But Andrew caught her by the arm.

'Don't, Kate,' he urged. 'You'll only make matters worse. They'll think you're guilty if you do that, and you wouldn't get far. You'll just have to go with him while I try and get help.'

'Is he arresting you too?' demanded Kate.

Andrew made a quick enquiry in Greek and then shook his head. The policeman, bored with the whole affair, picked up the handcuffs again and took a step towards Kate.

'No!' she protested. 'Look, Andrew, tell him I'll come with him, but I don't want to wear those things. And please get help quickly! Fetch Philip—he'll know what to do.'

'I will,' promised Andrew. 'Don't worry, Kate. We'll have you out of there in a few hours.'

As the policeman led her away Kate twisted her head for a last, desperate view of her friend. She saw Andrew hammering on the door of the one taxi driver in the village, then a van blocked her view. Oh, Philip, she thought despairingly, come soon!

The police station was above the cake shop next to the tavern where Kate had often eaten dinner with the archaeological team. She could not rid herself of a weird sense of disbelief as she was shepherded past families sitting at tables under the grape arbour and up a flight of stairs. Once inside, the policeman confiscated her money belt, passport, airline ticket and photographic equipment, but allowed her to keep a paperback book that she had with her. Her lack of Greek and his lack of English made it impossible for him to question her very thoroughly, but he wrote some notes in a large leather-bound book, then unlocked a cell and ushered her inside.

Kate had never been inside a prison cell before and she wasn't impressed. The walls and ceilings were painted an ugly shade of chocolate-brown and the window was high up and barred. A single naked light bulb hung from the ceiling, and the lavatory was no more than a hole in the floor in one corner of the room. There was an iron bedstead, covered in a torn brown blanket, and a lumpy pillow. Otherwise the room was empty. Miserably Kate dropped the book on the bed and sat down beside it, but the blanket reeked so strongly of cigarette smoke that it made her feel nauseated. Rising to her feet again, she paced restlessly round the cell. If only Andrew and Philip would hurry! She could not possibly endure more than a few hours in this awful place.

But eleven o'clock came, and then midnight, and there was still no sign of rescue. Exhausted, Kate finally sank down on the bed and dozed fitfully. She woke with a start and blinked sleepily at her watch. Three-seventeen a.m. Her heart sank. What could possibly have gone wrong? Where could Andrew be? Lying back, she stared miserably at the ceiling, while her brain raced with fevered images of drug pushers ambushing Andrew on his way to Áyios Dimitrios. Or, even worse, police shoot-outs in the foyer of the Hotel Ariadne in which Philip fell to the floor with an ominous red stain spreading across his chest. Suddenly Kate froze. Never mind the drug pushers or the gunshot wounds! She had suddenly seen an enormous cockroach stalking across the ceiling of her cell. The most gigantic cockroach she had ever seen in her life, and it was marching directly above her head!

With a strangled cry Kate leapt off the bed. She was convinced the hideous creature was going to drop down on her at any moment, and she backed into the corner furthest away from it. For the next hour neither of them got any sleep as the cockroach marched overhead and Kate countermarched below, trying to stay out of its way. Then suddenly Kate's nightmare was realised. The creature leapt on her. There was an instant of frenzy as she brushed it off her leg and felt its shiny carapace against her fingers, then it fell to the floor. Kate leapt up, snatched at her shoe and crushed it frantically.

Trembling slightly, she stood up and realised that the battle was over. Somehow this ridiculous victory gave her new heart. The dingy cell with its smoky blanket and bare walls no longer seemed so horrifying. All she had to do was keep her spirits up and wait. Philip would come for her. With that comforting thought, she lay down on the bed and fell into a deep and dreamless sleep.

Kate's determination to keep up her spirits was severely tested over the next two days. Now and then she heard footsteps on the stairs, but it was never Philip. The police officer was kind enough in a restrained way, but the language barrier made any real conversation impossible. Most of the time Kate was simply left alone to struggle with her fears and hopes as best she could. And inevitably her thoughts centred on Philip.

Memories surged back of their first meeting the night of the earthquake. How calm and competent he had been, and yet how arrogant, infuriating and overbearing! Some frenzied electrical current had leapt into life between them from the very first moment. She remembered the haunting bouzouki music he had played at Ayía Sofía, the way he had kissed her and the way her body had thrilled beneath his touch. And then there was the dinner at Porto Carras, when he had talked of his hopes and dreams for the village of his childhood. And she had responded by laying all her plans and ambitions before him. It was as if we knew right from the beginning that we were meant for each other, thought Kate despairingly. As if nothing could ever destroy the bond between us.

Except that everything seemed to have conspired to do exactly that. There had been so many obstacles in the way of their love. Quarrels, misunderstandings, interference from other people. And yet somehow Kate had always believed that the overwhelming emotion that tied them together would carry them safely through. Deep down she had no doubt whatever that Philip was the only man in the world for her, but did he also believe that she was the only woman for him? After two days without a word from him, her faith was beginning to waver.

Late on the second day of her imprisonment, she finally made a bitter admission to herself: Philip wasn't going to come and save her. He simply didn't care enough. In fact he had probably gone back to Irene by now. Up until this moment Kate had scarcely rested at all, expecting any moment to hear the knock at the door that would signal her release. But now she flung herself down on the bed, sobbed until the pillow was wet with tears and then fell into an exhausted sleep.

She was woken a couple of hours later by the grating of the door-handle. Assuming it was only the policeman with a trayful of food that she didn't intend to eat, she lay listlessly with her eyes closed and her face to the wall. Then suddenly a powerful pair of arms closed around her.

'Katarina!' said a deep, husky voice. 'Can you ever forgive me?'

Two hours later and still incoherent with bliss, Kate found herself tucked up in the front seat of Philip's white Saab, cruising through the starlit darkness of northern Sithoniá.

'I still can't believe this is real,' she murmured with a stifled yawn. 'I keep thinking that if I fall asleep you'll vanish.'

'I won't vanish,' he promised, reaching over and patting her knee. 'And I think a sleep would do you good.'

She nestled dreamily into the woven Greek rug that wrapped her comfortably.

'Explain it all to me again,' she begged. 'I'm not sure I understood it the first time.'

'Wait until we get to where we're going,' ordered Philip.

'Where are we going?'

'You'll see.'

She did sleep after that, and when she woke she found herself in a small whitewashed village. Dogs barked mournfully and a street-lamp sent the elongated shadows of a fig tree dancing on a high wall. The seat beside her was empty, and for one dreadful moment Kate thought that Philip had abandoned her. Then she saw the sign on the door of the house opposite. 'DOMATIA ENOIKIAZONTAI'. Rooms to let.

'Ayía Sofía!' cried Kate in delight as Philip came striding across the road towards her. 'You've brought me back to Ayía Sofía!'

'It's the one place in Greece where I didn't think the reporters would find us,' he agreed. 'And the landlady only remembers me as the poor man who was stranded here on the night of the earthquake. Although she did ask me how my pretty little wife was.'

Kate grinned.

'Well, *agapimou*, are you fit enough to go inside?' demanded Philip.

'Oh, yes!' agreed Kate. 'In fact, I think I'd kill for a shower and a hot meal right now.'

Philip smiled as they entered the whitewashed house, and gave her a gentle push.

'Well, you go and take the shower and I'll organise the meal,' he ordered. 'Oh, you'll want some fresh clothes. You'd better take these. They are just a few things I picked up for you in Paris.'

He thrust a very elegant paper carrier bag into her hand.

'Paris?' echoed Kate, watching his departing back. 'Oh, never mind!'

After the interior of the police cell, the tiny bathroom looked positively luxurious to Kate. It was sheer heaven to rotate under the warm spray of the shower and feel all the grime of the previous days being sluiced away. When at last she wrapped a towel around herself and padded into the bedroom, she felt an exhilaration beyond measure. Whatever else might be wrong, at least she and Philip were back together where they belonged. After rubbing her hair briskly she set down the towel and opened the carrier-bag. Her fingers met tissue paper, and she shook the contents out on to the bed. Then her eyes widened. A shimmering evening dress in green silk with matching handmade underwear, silk stockings, silver sandals and pearl earrings and necklace. Bought by Philip in Paris? But how? Why? Baffled beyond measure, Kate picked up the lace-trimmed jade teddy and began to dress.

When she emerged on to the terrace fifteen minutes later Philip was standing outlined against the shimmering silver backdrop of the sea. He turned and caught his breath as she came towards him.

'You look magnificent,' he said softly. 'Just the way I've always pictured you.'

Kate smiled.

'Thank you,' she murmured. 'But, Philip, what were you doing in Paris?'

'First things first,' insisted Philip.

He drew back her chair for her and bent foward to plant a warm kiss on her naked shoulder. Kate shivered with pleasure.

'Retsina?' he asked.

'Yes, please.'

She sipped the pale straw-coloured wine with its strange aroma of pine needles, and flashed a warm smile at Philip. He was sitting opposite her now, and he looked more attractive than ever with the lamplight burnishing his hair and lending fierce highlights to the sculpted angles of his face. Reaching across the table, Kate let her fingers trail over the fine dark hairs on the back of his lean brown hand.

'Thank you for the clothes,' she said with a hint of a question in her voice.

His low, vibrant laugh echoed round the terrace.

'And you'd like to know what the hell I was doing in Paris buying you clothes while you were languishing in prison?' he responded. 'It's a long story, my love. I'll tell you over dinner.'

At that moment Kyria Georgia appeared with a platter of hot pitta bread, charcoal-grilled octopus and assorted dips. Only when Kate had done full justice to these dishes did Philip speak again. As the *kyria* cleared away the empty plates he drew a folded piece of paper out of his pocket and handed it across the table to Kate.

'This is for you, too,' he said tersely.

Kate unfolded the paper and peered at it in the dim light.

'I don't understand!' she exclaimed. 'This is a bank cheque for a hundred thousand dollars.'

'Compensation,' agreed Philip. 'I tracked down Leon Clark at Stardust International and threatened to sue them for libelling you. They agreed to settle out of court. I thought a hundred thousand was an appropriate figure, since that was the amount he was pretending to have paid you for your story.'

'Pretending?' echoed Kate. 'Then you do believe that I didn't sell it to him, Philip?'

Philip took a swift gulp of his wine.

'Yes, I believe you,' he admitted. 'I think I always did, deep down, but I was so jealous of that swine that I was prepared to believe anything, no matter how ridiculous. And he did handle it all very cunningly. He made it appear as if he'd done the interview with you and then pocketed the fee himself.'

Kate stared at him, aghast.

'He actually admitted that to you?' she demanded.

'Oh, yes. He was extremely co-operative once I offered to strangle him with my bare hands.'

Kate choked with laughter.

'You barbarian!' she exclaimed. 'All the same, he deserved it!'

'He certainly did,' agreed Philip in a hard voice. 'If only for seducing you when he was already married to another woman. Katarina, why didn't you tell me about all that? If I'd known about that episode in your past perhaps I wouldn't have reacted so violently when I read that wretched article.'

Kate flushed uncomfortably under his gaze.

'I was afraid to tell you,' she admitted. 'You just assumed that I was a virgin, and I didn't want to disillusion you. And I suppose I was afraid you'd leave me if you knew.'

Philip's hand caught hers in a grip so hard that it was almost painful.

'I might have,' he admitted, 'but I wouldn't have stayed away for more than twenty-four hours. I love you, Katarina, and I can't pretend to be overjoyed that another man has possessed you in the past. But what matters to me now is the future. And I want to hear you say that I will be the only man in your life from now on.'

Kate's fingers fluttered nervously, and she gave a low, shaky laugh.

'Well, of course you will,' she murmured self-consciously.

'Say it,' ordered Philip implacably, still gripping her fingers. 'Swear it to me.'

She darted a swift glance at him and saw that he was totally serious. His liquid dark eyes blazed like candles in his face, and his expression was solemn. Suddenly her own embarrassment fell away, and she lifted her head and looked at him squarely.

'I swear that you will be the only man in my life from now on,' she said clearly.

He caught her hand and kissed it.

'And I swear that you will be the only woman in mine,' he responded.

They were still sitting with their hands entwined, gazing at each other, when Kyria Georgia appeared. She set down a plate of sizzling doner kebabs and a salad of tomatoes, olive, cucumber and feta cheese, and they both came back to earth. Kate helped herself to a couple of the aromatic skewers of meat, and smiled warmly at the older woman.

'Oraia,' she complimented her. *'Efharisto.'*

The Greek woman beamed as she withdrew.

The meat was tender, juicy and flavoured with aromatic herbs, and for several minutes they both turned their attention to eating. But at last Kate sat back with a sigh.

'That was delicious!' she said. 'But there are still some things I don't understand. Philip, did Leon tell you how he got into the house? He didn't really break in with a nail-file, did he?'

'No,' replied Philip. 'Stavros let him in.'

'Stavros?'

'Yes. And you, my little love, lied through your teeth to me. You told me that you didn't let Stavros inside the house, but you did, didn't you?'

Kate shifted uncomfortably under his stern gaze and then nodded.

'Why did you lie to me?' asked Philip grimly.

'I don't know,' said Kate in a troubled voice. 'You were so tired and cross that night you came back from Thessaloníki, and you seemed absolutely furious just because I'd played tennis with Stavros. It didn't seem worth starting another argument about the fact that he'd been inside the house. Especially when he'd done no harm there.'

'No harm!' sighed Philip, closing his eyes and pressing his fingers to his forehead. 'Oh, Kate, that's the understatement of the year.'

'Well, I didn't know then that he'd let Leon in,' retorted Kate defensively. 'Why on earth did he do that anyway?'

'Because he was determined to ruin you in my eyes,' replied Philip grimly. 'He knew how I hated reporters, so when Leon came sniffing around for a story it wasn't difficult for Stavros to hatch a plan that suited both of them. Stavros wormed his way inside, then left a window open for Leon and carried you off for a game of tennis so that Leon could search the house to his heart's content for your private letters and photos.'

Kate stared at him in horror.

'But that's despicable!' she cried. 'Anyway, why on earth would Stavros want to do such a thing to me?'

Philip's face set into a tense mask of lines and angles.

'I think he hoped that by discrediting you he would drive me back to Irene,' he replied.

'And he really thought she was so much in love with you that he was prepared to destroy me in order to bring you back together?' asked Kate.

Philip gave a mirthless laugh.

'No,' he said steadily. 'I'm sure Stavros realised that Irene felt nothing but indifference towards me. It was his own interests he was trying to protect, not hers. As his future brother-in-law, I've been bailing him out of trouble and paying his debts for years. He knew that would stop if I married you.'

'Debts?' repeated Kate. 'But Stavros is rich, isn't he?'

'Yes and no,' replied Philip. 'Old Con Marmara was nobody's fool, and he was very worried about his son's character. Before he died he made a will which tied up all Stavros's assets in a trust until he reached the age of thirty. I was the chief trustee, so Stavros was very dependent on my goodwill. And he knew that my sense of family honour would make me cover up his worst escapades if I were married to Irene. But not if I married you. So he was quite ruthless about trying to destroy you.'

Kate gave a small, shaky sigh.

'I can't believe it,' she said. 'Stavros always seemed so nice. So charming.'

'Well, his charm won't do him much good now,' retorted Philip drily. 'I don't think any judge will consider it an adequate defence for the possession of heroin.'

'Heroin?' cried Kate.

'Yes, haven't you figured it out yet?' said Philip. 'When you left Áyios Dimitrios, Stavros paid someone to follow you and plant the talcum-powder tin in your luggage. He also concealed heroin in our bedroom at Áyios Dimitrios to try and discredit you.'

'What?' demanded Kate.

'He wasn't taking any chances,' explained Philip wearily. 'One way or another he was determined to frame you. What I would like to know is why on earth you ever let him into our bedroom to plant the stuff.'

Kate blushed delicately.

'It was because of Irene's necklace,' she said in a low voice.

'Irene's necklace? What the hell are you talking about?' retorted Philip.

'The diamond necklace you gave her on the night of the hotel opening. Stavros said Irene had left it in your room when she stayed there overnight.'

Philip choked on his wine.

'And you believed that?' he demanded angrily.

Kate nodded miserably. 'He showed me the necklace,' she said.

'And were you in the room when he found it?' demanded Philip.

Kate thought back. 'No, I wasn't,' she said slowly.

Philip snorted impatiently. 'Of course you weren't,' he said, 'because that was just another bit of Stavros's low cunning, designed to drive a wedge between us. Irene didn't leave her necklace there when she slept with me because she's never slept with me in her life.'

'Truly?' asked Kate huskily.

'Truly,' insisted Philip.

A warm glow seemed to spread through Kate's entire body.

'I'm glad,' she said softly. 'Philip, you didn't really think I'd use heroin, did you?'

'Of course not!' said Philip emphatically. 'Stavros really over-played his hand there. Not that I was even there when the police found it, but they phoned me in Paris and asked me about it. And apparently they questioned Anna Vassiliou, the chambermaid, very closely about your habits. I'm told Anna was extremely indignant about the slur on your character, denied vigorously that you would do such a thing, and told them that in any case you were allergic to talcum powder.'

Kate smiled.

'Dear Anna,' she said. 'But, Philip, you still haven't told me what you were doing in Paris!'

'Apart from buying underwear for you?' teased Philip. 'Well, I'll tell you, Katarina. I was negotiating with a new backer for the Hotel Ariadne.'

'What?' cried Kate. 'Oh, Philip, with all that's been happening I'd forgotten all about that! Did you succeed?'

Philip swirled his wine in his glass with the intent, excited look of a master chess-player about to make his final move.

'Yes,' he said.

'So the Hotel Ariadne is safe?' insisted Kate.

'Yes. After all the panic and uproar, I think the hotel and the village can look forward to living happily ever after,' he said with a contented sigh. 'Rather like us, I suppose.'

He rose to his feet and stretched out his hand to Kate.

'Come and look at the moon over the water,' he invited.

Every nerve in her body quivered at the touch of that warm brown hand on her skin. When they sat down together on the parapet she leaned against him, revelling in his powerful male presence. His breath stirred her hair, she could smell the spicy aroma of his cologne and his arms were warm and comforting about her.

'Look!' he said softly. 'It's so clear tonight that you can see all the way across to Mount Áthos.'

Kate shielded her eyes against the silvery, shimmering radiance of the moonlight and, sure enough, there behind the brightness were the dark, razor-edged peaks of the holy peninsula.

'Isn't it beautiful?' she breathed.

'Doubly beautiful when you are here to share it with me,' replied Philip softly.

Kyria Georgia came out at that moment with a tray of fresh fruit and coffee. She stopped and smiled fondly at the couple on the terrace. Then, coming forward, she murmured something to Philip.

'What did she say?' asked Kate.

'She asked if I'd like to borrow the bouzouki again,' said Philip with a smile. 'After all, what's a moonlit night without music? *Nai, nai, efharisto, Kyria.*'

After they had finished their coffee and fruit, the Kyria came back with the graceful honey-gold instrument in her hands. For the next hour Kate listened entranced while Philip played haunting love-songs, wild dance music and traditional laments. But at last he laid aside the bouzouki and cupped her face in his hands.

'I'm sorry we quarrelled at Áyios Dimitrios,' he said huskily. 'It was my fault.'

Kate smiled and her hands moved up and covered his.

'It doesn't matter,' she assured him, trailing her fingers along the dark hair on the backs of his hands.

He gave a faint groan and she saw the sudden flare of desire in his eyes.

'When we were here last time you asked me what would happen if you were really my wife and we quarrelled. Do you remember?'

Kate nodded, feeling a delicious, tingling warmth spread slowly through her veins.

'You said the quarrel would certainly be settled in bed,' she whispered.

Philip's lips came down on hers, warm and fresh and persuasive. His kiss grew deeper and more urgent. She arched her back, moulding her body to his as he caught her savagely against him. At last he caught his breath and thrust her away from him.

'I think it's time our quarrel was settled,' he said hoarsely.

Taking her by the arm, he led her into the simple whitewashed bedroom. Slowly, almost reverently, he removed her elegant Parisian clothes until her lithe curves were exposed to his gaze. His fingers trembled as he reached out and touched the swelling mound of her breast.

'You are so beautiful, *agapimou*,' he murmured.

Fire leapt through her veins, and her entire body seemed to pulse with longing as his hands continued caressing her.

'I love you, Philip,' she said urgently as his lips moved down the slender column of her throat.

'I love you too, Katarina. More than I can ever tell you,' he replied huskily. 'Come, my darling, let me show you how much.'

Then somehow he was in bed beside her and his powerful, naked body was warm and urgent against her tender flesh. His strong hands sent quivers of desire shooting through her, and his lips were a torment of pleasure on her satiny skin. She nestled closer to him, sighing with need, and offering her own tentative caresses until at last they both went wild with longing and moved together in a rhythm of passion as old as time. Again and again he brought her to the peak of ecstasy, and then at last he tensed and cried out, clutching her against him and moaning her name. And an overwhelming peace and contentment descended on them both.

Later on they lay sleepily entwined, enjoying the mingled warmth and closeness of their bodies, Kate reached up and stroked his springy dark hair.

'Philip?' she murmured blissfully.

'Mmm?'

'It's funny, isn't it? When we stayed here the first time and you pretended I was your wife for a night I couldn't help wondering what it would be like to be your wife forever.'

He smiled and nuzzled her cheek. Then his lips alighted on her closed eyelids. First one, then the other.

'Well, you'll soon know, *agapimou*,' he promised tenderly.

Then, reaching across her, he switched out the light.

HARLEQUIN ◆ PRESENTS®

BARBARY WHARF

Home to the *Sentinel*
Home to passion, heartache and love

Charlotte Lamb

The BARBARY WHARF six-book saga concludes with Book Six, SURRENDER. The turbulent relationship between Nick Caspian and Gina Tyrrell reaches its final crisis. Nick is behaving like a man possessed, and he claims Gina's responsible. She may have declared war on him, but one thing is certain— Nick has never surrendered to anyone in his life and he's not about to start now. Will this final battle bring Nick and Gina together, or will it completely tear them apart?

**SURRENDER (Harlequin Presents #1540)
available in March.**

October: BESIEGED (#1498)
November: BATTLE FOR POSSESSION (#1509)
December: TOO CLOSE FOR COMFORT (#1513)
January: PLAYING HARD TO GET (#1522)
February: A SWEET ADDICTION (#1530)

Where do you find hot Texas nights, smooth Texas charm and dangerously sexy cowboys?

COWBOYS AND CABERNET

Raise a glass—Texas style!

Tyler McKinney is out to prove a Texas ranch is the perfect place for a vineyard. Vintner Ruth Holden thinks Tyler is too stubborn, too impatient, too...Texas. And far too difficult to resist!

CRYSTAL CREEK reverberates with the exciting rhythm of Texas. Each story features the rugged individuals who live and love in the Lone Star State. And each one ends with the same invitation...

Y'ALL COME BACK...REAL SOON!

Don't miss *COWBOYS AND CABERNET* by Margot Dalton. Available in April wherever Harlequin books are sold.